He had to get to her.

He looked up the cliff. "Theresa? I'm on my way up."

No answer. Snow fell heavily, and the wind beat against him. For every step, he slid back three. Where was she? A shiver of fear brushed his spine. "Theresa? You there?"

All he heard in response was a scream for help that filled his heart with dread. Theresa was in danger.

"Hold on! I'm coming!"

He scrambled to the top, his heart pounding like a fist inside his rib cage. He tried to get around the car that hovered over the cliff, but he couldn't catch his grip.

"Alex, help!" Her voice floated on the wind.

He grabbed the twisted bumper and hoisted himself up onto the hood. The unstable car groaned beneath him, and he knew he'd have only one shot to save himself. He leaped for the branch above him at the same time the car plunged into the frozen lake.

And then he heard it. The deafening, unmistakable sound of a gunshot.

Maggie K. Black is an award-winning journalist and romantic suspense author with an insatiable love of traveling the world. She has lived in the American South, Europe and the Middle East. She now makes her home in Canada with her history-teacher husband, their two beautiful girls and a small but mighty dog. Maggie enjoys connecting with her readers at maggiekblack.com.

Books by Maggie K. Black

Love Inspired Suspense

True North Bodyguards

Kidnapped at Christmas
Rescue at Cedar Lake

Killer Assignment
Deadline
Silent Hunter
Headline: Murder
Christmas Blackout
Tactical Rescue

Visit the Author Profile page at Harlequin.com.

RESCUE AT CEDAR LAKE

MAGGIE K. BLACK

HARLEQUIN® LOVE INSPIRED® SUSPENSE

Recycling programs
for this product may
not exist in your area.

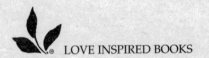

LOVE INSPIRED BOOKS

ISBN-13: 978-0-373-67806-8

Rescue at Cedar Lake

Copyright © 2017 by Mags Storey

www.Harlequin.com

Printed in U.S.A.

There is a time for everything, and a season for every activity under the heavens: a time to tear and a time to mend, a time to be silent and a time to speak.
—*Ecclesiastes* 3:1, 7

With thanks to my amazing agent, Melissa Jeglinski, my wonderful editor, Emily Rodmell, the whole Love Inspired team and the incredible group of other Love Inspired writers who encourage me onward in the battle to turn stories into words.

I am very grateful to be surrounded by so many strong and talented women. You inspire me.

ONE

Alex Dean fixed his sharp blue eyes on the screen of his Ash Private Security laptop and prayed hard for his stepsister, Zoe, to answer the secure video call. Winter winds howled through the trees outside and shook the frost-covered windows of the Dean family cottage. A storm was coming. The video call kept ringing. He ran his hand over the back of his neck where sandy blond hair brushed the collar of his leather jacket. Where was she?

Zoe wasn't just family. She was a colleague and fellow bodyguard who'd joined him in helping their boss, Daniel Ash, create Ash Private Security. Despite being four foot eleven, she was every bit as strong and savvy a fighter as the rest of the team. Not to mention her assignment had been a very simple one—to bring a stressed-out university student up to the remote shores of Cedar Lake,

Ontario, for a weekend of quiet studying. Not a high risk assignment by any means. The twenty-year-old client, Mandy Rhodes, came from one of the high-powered families they'd grown up knowing because their families all had cottages at the isolated lake. She was also the second cousin of their close friend Joshua, who was overseas completing his final few months of military service.

But after the initial check-in call yesterday, Zoe had fallen out of contact. He hadn't been able to get through to her last night. Then, when Alex had called again this morning to give her a heads-up that a vicious, unexpected storm now threatened to wreak havoc on the roads and send power lines crashing down, Zoe still hadn't answered. Cedar Lake had never had reliable cell phone service, though. Even the state-of-the-art Wi-Fi hotspots on their laptops had glitched far too often. So he'd driven up in person to double-check everything was okay—and found the cottage empty.

Empty and yet oddly tidy. There were no signs of a struggle. Or that Zoe and Mandy had ever made it there. Instead, the rustic space where he'd spent his childhood summers almost looked like it'd been gone over by a professional cleaning service. Something he might've taken comfort in if Mandy's parents hadn't warned them she was so stressed out about university that the last time they'd let her come up alone to study, just a couple of weeks ago, she'd left her family cottage in such a bad state they weren't about to let her travel up alone again. And he'd never known Zoe to be anything close to neat.

Unlike Theresa Vaughan.

He winced as his ex-fiancée's captivating green eyes suddenly flickered across his mind. Theresa was the only person he'd ever known with the compulsion to leave every place she touched more beautiful than she'd found it—something some of the other kids on the lake had teased her about. The stunning brunette's wealthy family owned the large cottage at the mouth of the lake. Their romance had first blossomed as teenagers when he'd been watching with his buddies from a cottage window as a thunderstorm capsized her sailboat. Her harness had gotten tangled in the rigging, trapping her underwater. While the other kids had laughed, oblivious to the danger she was in, Alex had pelted down the shore, barely pausing to kick off his shoes before he'd leaped off the dock and swum to her rescue. She was now a trauma counselor and psychotherapist who also worked with Ontario Victim Services, and remained the one and only person Alex had ever pledged his foolish heart to—even though she'd broken that heart and called off their engagement just days before the wedding.

The computer beeped. He looked up. The call had timed out. He hit Redial. Alex drummed his fingers on the table. The call icon circled on the screen. Was a suspiciously clean cottage all it took to distract him with thoughts of Theresa? Despite putting eight and a half years between himself and that summer, the memory of losing her still ached like an old scar at the edges of his heart. This was why he hadn't been back to the lake since that day, no matter how many times his family and friends had urged him to come. Every inch was a minefield of unwanted memories, from the huge rocks in front of her cottage where he'd proposed, to the apartment over the boathouse—where he'd thrown the returned engagement ring so hard it had gotten lost under the floorboards.

The call to Zoe stopped again. He hit Redial for a second time. Then his head dropped into his hands, and he shoved his sore memories to the furthest reaches of his mind. It would only be a matter of time before the impending storm took out the power lines and cut off road access. If he didn't leave soon, he could be stuck there in the cold, remote cottage without power for days. His sister and their client's safety mattered. Nothing else.

"Hello? Alex?" A voice filled the air. Puzzled. Female. But it wasn't his sister's. No, this voice was both sweet and strong like the first coffee waking him up in the morning. "Hello? Can you hear me?"

He blinked. "Theresa?"

He looked up at the screen. Theresa sat on a chair in front of his sister's laptop with a slightly concerned look on her face and the snow-filled windows of a different cottage in the background. Long dark hair tumbled around her shoulders in the kind of disheveled, messy way he'd always found adorable. A question hovered in her deep green eyes. She was engulfed by a giant red sweatshirt with "Canada" embroidered across it in big block letters, but because of the way the fabric fell it almost seemed to read "and." Hang on. Wasn't that one of *his* old sweatshirts?

"What's going on?" he asked. "Where's Zoe and Mandy?"

"Not here." Theresa said. Her nose wrinkled. "I'm guessing Zoe hasn't managed to call you yet. They left me at Mandy's family's cottage and went for a drive to find a cell phone signal and pick up some groceries about an hour ago. Mandy is supposed to be hitting the books and staying offline. But once we got here, she was really panicked about not being able to surf the internet or get a cell phone signal. So I told Zoe it might be best not to make a video or use the laptop around her. Zoe said it wouldn't be a problem, that you'd understand, and she'd call you this morning to explain. I got out the laptop after they left. When the call kept ringing and ringing I figured it might be important."

He sighed heavily. "It is."

"And I presume Zoe didn't tell you she'd brought me in on this?"

"No, she didn't." He crossed his arms and leaned back in the chair. He wasn't sure what he thought of his former fiancée making decisions that impacted an active operation, especially if it kept him out of the loop.

Zoe and Theresa had reconnected at Christmas, after Theresa and Samantha, a journalist she was working with, had been violently threatened. That had been the first thread that had relinked Alex's life to Theresa's. Since then there'd been even more. His best friend, Josh, was now engaged to Samantha, Alex was going to be their best man, and he'd already been warned that Theresa was invited to the wedding. Josh was also joining Ash Private Security when his tour of duty was up and had made it clear he thought Theresa's unique perspective on crime victims would make her a strong asset to their team. Both Zoe and Daniel agreed and had already asked Theresa to advise on a few clients.

So far, all Alex had said on the matter was that he was fine with it and they all had his blessing to work with her. Just as long as he didn't have to see her or talk to her until he was ready.

Now, ready or not, here she was.

"I don't understand why Zoe needed to bring you in," he said, "just because our client's dealing with a little bit of stress."

"Not everyone's able to just shrug away stress and ignore it." Her arms crossed, too, mirroring his stance. "Mandy's not in a good place right now. She's emotionally frazzled. Remember, both her brothers are a lot older and very successful."

Mandy's twin brothers were a year older

than Alex, and had always been arrogant, athletic and entitled. True, as adults they'd done well for themselves. Emmett now owned a string of fancy car dealerships. Kyle was a local politician.

"Being under pressure is part of being young," he said. It was hardly a crisis.

"Maybe," Theresa went on. "But her parents are pretty overprotective and I'm getting the suspicion that there's something more going on. Not that she's been willing to open up to me about it yet."

Well, Mandy's breakdown would have to wait until the storm was over. He got why that kind of stuff might matter to a psychotherapist like Theresa. But it didn't make much difference to his mission to get everyone home safely. His temples ached as his brain tried to translate everything she'd told him into a workable solution. There were several different towns in the area Zoe could've driven to. His options were to wait for them to get back, try to go find them, or just get somewhere with a functional cell signal and try to call Zoe again.

"And you're at Mandy's parents' cottage now?" he confirmed.

"Yeah, Number Eight Cedar Lake, on the

far side. Not one of her brother's properties. I know originally the plan had been for us to stay at your family's cottage. But Mandy was getting too stir-crazy and said she wanted to be somewhere familiar, so I suggested we move over here."

Which now put her over forty-five minutes away by truck in weather like this. Though, if the early winter had been colder and the lake had frozen over properly, he could've grabbed his snowmobile from the boathouse and been there in fifteen minutes. But, as it was, the risk of hitting a thin patch in the middle was just too high. He ran his hand along his jaw, oddly thankful he'd shaved that morning. Theresa had never liked him in a beard.

Enough talk. He had to make a decision. "Where's your car?"

"Back home. Zoe picked me up from the bus station."

"Well, I'm sorry to cut your weekend therapy session short, but there's a really bad storm coming. Several inches of snow falling this afternoon followed by a bunch of freezing rain tonight. Her parents asked us to bring her home. Emmett called my cell phone, berated me for even letting her come up here without running it by him, and threatened to come up and collect her himself personally if I didn't bring her home right away." Then he'd called back a second time and left a voice mail message saying that he'd sue Ash into the ground if anything happened to Mandy. "You two can talk while we drive or pick things up again once we're out of harm's way. But a storm this bad could take down whole trees, killing the power and blocking off the roads. I'll drive around the lake to join you. Then, as soon as Zoe and Mandy get back, we'll all head out together."

"I can tell you right now that Mandy won't want to leave here if she thinks this is something her family is forcing on her," Theresa said. Her voice was gentle, but there was still an edge to it that made him envision her heels digging into the floorboards. "She wants to be up here. Granted, she wasn't prepared for losing her phone and internet connection. But that doesn't mean she wanted to go home. This is Canada. Cottages withstand winter storms all the time. A few quiet days studying by candlelight and heating soup over the fire is probably the best thing for Mandy. More importantly, she needs to be able to decide for herself what happens next. Not to be told what to do. Or pressured into a dangerous drive on short notice."

"I hear you, but that's not your call to make," he said. "Her parents hired Ash Private Security to look after her. They didn't trust her traveling alone and they don't much like the idea of her being cut off from the world in a dark and cold cottage."

"Not even if she thinks it's what's best for her?" Theresa asked.

There was the distant hum of a motor outside and it took him a moment to realize it was coming from Theresa's end of the call. Sounded like Zoe and Mandy were back. Thankfully.

"She's twenty." Alex's eyes rolled. "She doesn't know what she wants. She'll probably change her mind the moment we're on the highway."

Theresa frowned. Okay, he probably shouldn't have put it like that. But she was the last person who was going to convince him that what someone thought at twenty was a deciding factor in what they would or wouldn't do. When she called off the wedding she'd been twenty, he'd been twenty-one and the argument had been such a mess he still wasn't sure how it had happened. He'd told her he'd decided to drop out of university because, while a full scholarship was great and all, he wasn't sure he wanted to study medicine. She'd said something about her parents having money problems, and that he needed to grow up, step up and be more responsible. The next thing he knew she was dropping the ring back into his hand.

"Look, I'm not trying to start a fight," Theresa said. "Zoe tells me you're really great at the whole bodyguard thing. I'm just asking you to take the time to think through how you're going to talk to Mandy about this. This is no time for you to just charge ahead and not think about the consequences."

By which she meant what, exactly?

There was banging and rattling behind her like someone trying to get the porch doors open. He looked past her, but all he could see were the shifting silhouettes of figures behind the glass.

"Hang on," Theresa said. "They've probably locked themselves out. I'll let Zoe know you're on the call and then she can take over talking to you."

"Great. Thanks." He was almost positive Zoe would side with him.

Alex watched Theresa's hair swish and

fall down her back as she walked toward the door. Her wool socks padded softly on the hardwood floor. The sweatshirt swamped her slender body down to her jeans-clad thighs. A long breath left his lungs. Even more than eight years later and through the unflattering lens of a laptop webcam, she was still every bit as beautiful as she'd always been. Theresa paused at the patio door. There were three figures standing at the large glass doors, all of whom were too big to be either Zoe or Mandy.

They exchanged words he couldn't quite make out. Then Theresa's back straightened so sharply it sent fear coursing down his own spine.

"Hey!" he called, hoping the volume on the laptop was up high enough that she could hear him. "Is everything okay?"

The distorted sound of the men shouting crackled through the speakers. They started banging on the glass. Worry now pooled at the base of his spine. Did she have anything to defend herself with? His eyes scanned the room. A fake antique bayonet and decorative sword were crossed over the mantel, but even at a glance he could tell how useless they would both be in a real battle. But she might be able to barricade herself in a room upstairs long enough for him to help her plan an escape.

"Theresa! Listen to me!" His voice rose. "Don't panic. I can help you protect yourself. But you need to do exactly what I say."

Theresa took a step back, but her head didn't turn. The shouting grew louder and more vulgar, with the demand that she open the door. The glass windows and doors rattled and shook like an earthquake.

"Theresa!" He forced his voice to stay clear and calm even as he battled the fear beating in his chest. "I need you to listen to me. Step away from the window. Walk backward to the laptop. Then grab a piece of furniture. Heavy but something you can lift. A small table. A chair."

She wasn't listening. Her eyes darted to the weapons above the fireplace.

Dear God, please help me protect her!

Her hands struggled in vain to pull the antique weapons down from the brackets holding them.

"Theresa! Please! Listen to me!"

Oh Lord, please, save her life.

The patio door splintered. Theresa turned and ran toward the laptop. But she'd barely taken a step before the world exploded behind her. Wood splintered. Glass shattered. Wind whipped through the open doorway, hurling snow in with it. Three men ran through in winter jackets, blue jeans and ski masks.

Armed with shotguns.

A scream ripped from Theresa's lips. Her fingers reached toward the keyboard.

Someone grabbed her from behind. The laptop fell to the floor. It landed on its side and for one helpless moment Alex could see nothing but muddy floorboards and boots. Then Theresa's head hit the ground. A gloved hand pushed her against the floor.

Theresa's panicked face filled the screen. Her terrified eyes met his.

Theresa's lungs ached with every breath. A hand gripped the back of her head pushing the side of her face into the floor. A knee pressed hard into the small of her back.

Alex's eyes met hers through the screen of the fallen laptop. She could hear the men searching the cottage. Things were being tossed off shelves. Furniture clattered and fell. Male voices shouted and swore. She kept her eyes locked on Alex like a lifeline. Alex leaped to his feet, still holding the laptop in one hand while he dialed his cell phone with the other.

"Stay strong, Theresa," his voice filtered faintly through the speakers. Fear filled his blue eyes, making something inside her own chest ache in pain. "I'm coming for you. I promise."

A boot landed hard on the laptop, stomping it over and over again until the screen died. Alex's face disappeared. She was alone. Theresa closed her eyes and prayed. *Lord, help me. Please. Whatever this is, please keep Zoe and Mandy safe from it. Thank You that Alex knows I'm in trouble. But please, keep him out of danger.*

His cottage was a good forty-five minutes' drive from here. The nearest police station was more than an hour and a half away. Even if Alex came for her, would she even be here when he arrived? Would she even still be alive? Panic filled her throat pushing tears to her eyes.

Mandy had seemed so anxious and distracted about something. Did it have something to do with these men? If so, how had Theresa missed it? Dealing with victims of violent crime was a huge part of her work and yet she'd never imagined Mandy could be linked to something like this.

"Castor!" A voice filtered down from the second floor landing. "It's not here!"

"Well it's somewhere!" The man pinning her down shouted loudly. "Tear the place apart if you have to!" His hand jabbed in the direction of a small, wooden hatch, barely visible in the floor near the kitchen's old-fashioned wood-burning stove. "Check the cold cellar. Check everywhere. If they've got it, they'll have brought it here."

A heavy man in a red ski mask yanked the hatch open. "There's nothing down there. Just wood and kindling."

"Then check upstairs." Her captor growled in frustration. Then he yanked her head back. His low, menacing voice filled her ear. "Where's the trunk?"

"What trunk?" She tried to turn her head toward him but his grip held her tight. "Look, this isn't my cottage. I don't know what you're talking about."

"We're looking for a trunk!" Castor shouted, so loudly her ears rang. His mouth grew even closer to her face. The stench of stale coffee and cigars grew stronger as he leaned toward her, shifting his weight deeper onto her torso. "You know, a large, heavy, old-fashioned luggage trunk. Something big enough to hide a body in."

Snickering came from the other side of the room.

"Again, this isn't my cottage!" She could almost feel the defiance rising in her voice, battling back against the fear as her breath pushed its way out of her aching lungs. "I just got here this morning. I haven't seen a trunk."

Castor sat back, relieving just enough of the pressure on her torso to let her gasp a deeper breath. He turned and shouted more frustrated profanities at his two henchmen. For a moment, she was ignored again as they ransacked Mandy's family cottage. She closed her eyes, prayers filling her heart as she listened and tried to focus on any tiny sliver of information she could glean. Castor called the other two Brick and Howler. Brick sounded angry and frustrated by the futility of the search. Howler barely spoke.

"Where's Mandy Rhodes?" All too soon Castor was back barking in her ear again. "And that other woman she drove up with?"

A shiver of fear ran through her heart. How did he know who they were? Had they been watching them?

Lord, please keep Zoe and Mandy far, far away from here.

"I don't know where they are. They went for a drive."

"Where did they go?" Castor's grip tightened. "When are they getting back?"

"I don't know! They didn't tell me!"

Her hands were yanked back. She heard the rip of duct tape tearing. Then she felt him bind her wrists together behind her. Castor stood and pulled her to her feet. She looked up at the tall, heavyset man, whose sneering mouth and dangerous eyes seemed to float unmoored through the holes of a ski mask. "You'd better not be lying to me."

"I'm not. I can't tell you what I don't know."

Castor leaned in so close that his face was inches from her, making it difficult not to turn away from the stench of his hot breath. "What if I threaten to kill you, slowly and painfully? Would that help you remember?"

No. But it would make her even more determined to not go down without a fight. She head butted him, as hard as she could. His head snapped back as her forehead cracked hard against his jaw. He let go of her. She turned and sprinted across the wooden floor toward the shattered remains of the doorway. Melting puddles of snow seeped into her socks. A bracing winter wind brushed her face. A sharp pain filled her skull as Castor's rough hands grabbed her hair and snapped her backward. "Now I'm really going to make you hurt."

Lord, please. I need You now...

"Come on, dude! This is a waste of time!" The rail-thin masked man the others called Howler snorted loudly from the corner of the room. The sound that was halfway between a laugh and a snarl. He waved his shotgun in their direction. "This wasn't the job I signed up for. You want her dead? I'll kill her. Bang. Right now. No problem. Or if you can, kill her quick so we can move on. Whatever. You said we've got a trunk to find. All I care about is getting my cut of the money. And I don't wanna not get my money just because we're stuck here waiting while you punish that finicky little princess chick for not telling you what you want to know!"

Finicky little princess? Theresa blinked as the words clanged like old bells at the corner of her mind. But before she could decipher the ringing, Castor shoved her across the room. He pushed her into the broom closet. She fell, landing hard on her knees among the mops and cleaning supplies. Castor stood over her. Blood seeped through the mouth of the mask. Her head butt had split his lip. "Fine. We'll go find the trunk. But then I'm coming back and dealing with her when we're done. She knows something. I'm sure of it. It's in her memory somewhere. Even if she's too useless to remember it."

"Whatever," Howler said. "Do whatever you want to do. Just after I get my money."

The closet door slammed shut. Darkness fell. She heard a chair being scraped against the door.

"Brick!" Castor snapped. "Sit here. Watch the door. Shoot her if she tries to escape. But don't kill her. I might need her later."

There was a muffled argument and some more swearing that ended when Castor snapped that Brick would get an extra cut of payment at the end if he stayed behind to watch her, and a shotgun slug in the head if he didn't. Then there was the thud of a body landing in a chair against the door. Castor and Howler's voices faded away.

Theresa pulled herself into a seated position, slid a metal bucket behind her and scraped the duct tape binding her hands against the spout. It loosened slowly. Her socks were so wet and cold her feet stung. Theresa prayed hard, begging God to save her life and to protect Mandy, Zoe and Alex from danger. Then she took a deep breath and focused her mind on the criminals, pulling together the scraps of what she knew as if this was a file that she'd gotten through Victim Services.

These men were thieves. That much she knew. Castor and his lackeys were looking to steal some kind of trunk that he seemed to think she'd know about. But why? What could it hold that was worth ransacking a cottage over? Whatever it was, the henchmen were worried about running out of time and not getting their cut of the bounty. Castor had mentioned Mandy by name and knew about Zoe. So she couldn't rule out that it had something to do with Mandy's anxiety. But Theresa couldn't be sure. Both Mandy's older brothers were successful enough to have enemies.

Howler had called her a "finicky little princess."

She closed her eyes and worked her duct-taped hands faster against the pail as the words pricked at painful memories buried so deep in the recesses of her mind that she had to ease them out slowly, bit by bit, like getting burrs out of her hair. She'd almost managed to forget that some of the kids at Cedar Lake had called her "princess." They'd called her "useless," too, and other things implying they thought she was too pampered and non-athletic to ever be one of them. She didn't know who'd started it. But it'd definitely gotten worse after they'd seen her sailboat capsize in a sudden summer storm. She'd gotten tangled in the rigging and might've drowned if Alex hadn't come to her rescue.

Back then, her parents owned a large seasonal equipment store on the highway north of Toronto. It sold boats, personal watercraft, sporting goods, barbecues and cottage furniture, along with whole rooms of decorative country kitsch. As a family, they'd always had the newest and nicest toys on the lake—sample models to trial, mostly. At the end of every summer, one of the other families on the lake, the Wrights, would host a huge team scavenger hunt. Afterward, Theresa's mother would invite all the families on the lake over for barbecue.

That annual barbecue was also going be her wedding reception the summer she'd been twenty.

So, maybe there'd been some jealousy. Or

the misconception that her family had more money than they did. But just before she'd turned twenty a warehouse fire had wiped out most of their inventory. The family then lost a long, hard court battle, in which, because the security cameras apparently hadn't been working, the insurance company had accused her dad of setting the fire to cover some bad debts. So less than a month before her wedding, her parents realized they were probably going to go bankrupt and started making quiet plans to sell their business, cottage and home in a last-ditch effort to pay off their debts.

She could still remember the anxiety filling her heart as she'd gone to tell Alex. She'd been looking for a shoulder to cry on. Instead, he'd met her with the news that he'd dropped out of yet another university program, just tossing away a full scholarship and paid internship, as if real-world responsibilities didn't even matter.

But that was just the way Alex was. He was spontaneous. But that day he'd been so full of blather that her sadness had turned to frustration. She'd said maybe they should postpone the wedding until he grew up enough. They'd fought. He took the cruel taunt that the other kids made about how she seemed to think she was royalty and aimed it at her heart with an added sting: *should've known better than to fall for such a finicky little princess like you.*

She'd handed the ring back, feeling too hurt to even cry. And that had been that.

"I'm done waiting." Brick's voice snapped through the closed door. "I'm cold. This is stupid. I want my money. I'm going to go find the thing myself. But I don't know my way around this stupid lake and Castor thinks you know something. So you're going to help me, whether you want to or not."

The cupboard door flew open. With one desperate tug she yanked her hands free. Duct tape tore. The bucket clattered behind her. She launched herself headfirst into Brick, knocking him back so hard he slipped and hit the floor. He'd taken off his ski mask, showing a square face with fat cheeks, thin lips and deep-set eyes. She pushed past him and ran down the narrow hallway leading to the cottage's smaller back door. If she could just grab her boots and her gloves and make it out the back door she might be able to escape through the trees and find somewhere to hide.

A sawed-off shotgun blast sounded behind

her. Splinters exploded in the wall ahead as a hunting slug struck the wood.

"You keep running, I'll shoot you," Brick said. "Castor's made me put up with too much nonsense to stick me on babysitting duty. I need that trunk. I want my money. So, you're gonna help me find it. Even if you're bleeding and in pieces."

Her stocking feet froze beneath her as her brain struggled to think. Even if she cooperated, he was likely to kill her eventually, unless she just went along with him until she found a way to escape. But if she tried to keep running, she had no doubt he'd shoot her on the spot. There was a thud on the roof above them, like a sudden clump of snow falling off a tree branch. The hot barrel of a weapon brushed against the back of her head.

"I don't know anything about a trunk." Her hands rose slowly. "But I'll help you leave Cedar Lake if you promise not to hurt anyone else."

"Nice try." He snorted. "But I'm the boss now. We can do this the easy way or the hard way, but, either way, I'm not leaving this lake without what I came for. Castor said he was willing to pay me good to find this trunk. He'll probably pay me double if I find it first.

And if he gets mad at me for hurting you, I'll just tell him it's your fault for running away." He spun her around and marched her back into the remains of the living room. "Now, you're going to start cooperating. Because if ya don't, I'm going to hurt you so bad you're gonna wish I'd just shot ya."

An ugly grin spread across his flat face. She closed her eyes and prayed.

A crash sounded from the low roof above. Brick swore. She opened her eyes in time to see a snow-covered form in jeans, a brown leather jacket and snowmobile helmet swing down through the open doorway. Brick grabbed her hard around her neck and yanked her back in a headlock, pressing her body back tight against his like a hostage. The tip of the sawed-off shotgun pressed into the soft flesh at the base of her skull just behind her ear.

"Look man, whoever you are, I'm just a guy looking for the same thing you are!" Brick shouted. "The trunk's not here. We don't have it and we don't know where it is! So there's no need for any problems. Just turn around and pretend you never saw us."

"No can do." The man in leather moved

forward. "Drop your weapon, and I'll let you leave. But you're going to let her go."

He pulled off his helmet. Her breath caught in her throat.

It was Alex.

TWO

Theresa's jaw dropped as her former fiancé stepped toward her through the ransacked cottage. How was he here? It'd barely been twenty minutes since Castor and his thugs first attacked her. There was no way Alex could've driven around the lake in that amount of time, and the ice on the lake was hardly safe. Snowflakes clung to his body. Jeans and a leather jacket hung on his tall, muscular frame. A long scarf looped around his neck and hung all the way to his waist. His blue-eyed gaze brushed her face.

"Hey, Theresa." He took another step forward with that casual saunter of his that always made it look like he was all joints and yet totally comfortable in his skin. Brick tightened his grip. Alex stopped. His hands rose slightly. But his smile never faltered.

What was he doing, strolling casually toward the armed man who held her captive like he was some action hero?

"Look, clearly your buddies have taken off and left you all alone without any backup. So how about you drop that shotgun and we talk this out?" Alex asked. Something she'd never seen before flashed in his eyes, an edge that was as firm and unrelenting as steel. "Because there's no way I'm letting you hurt her."

The wind outside grew louder. The cottage seemed to shake on its foundations.

"I'm the one in charge here!" Bravado and uncertainty pushed through Brick's words in equal measure, and it wasn't clear which one was going to win. "Me! Not you. Not Castor. Not anyone! I'm going to take her with me and find that trunk, and nobody's going to stop me!"

Alex shrugged, and as he did his whole body seemed to shift forward in one smooth motion. "You sure about that?"

Panic crawled up Theresa's throat. Alex was going to get them both killed. He meant well. He was a great guy. But was he really equipped to handle any of this?

The headlock tightened until all she could feel was the pressure choking the oxygen from her lungs. "Look, man! I'm not playing! She's gonna die. I'm gonna kill her. You got that?"

"Loud and clear." Alex leaped. In one quick motion he struck the weapon away from Theresa's body and yanked Brick's arm around behind him. Theresa fell free and stumbled forward. Brick yelped in pain. Alex wrenched Brick's arm upward, using the pain and leverage to force him down onto the floor.

"Theresa, are you okay?" Alex stood over Brick. Concern filled his eyes as he searched her face. "Did he hurt you?"

She blinked. It had all happened so fast she'd barely been able to see it happening. But there Brick was, groaning on the floor, while Alex stood over him, keeping the huge thug down through pressure on his wrist alone. Her mind swam. This couldn't be happening. She must be dreaming. Her former fiancé had always been an athlete, and Zoe said he excelled at his private security training, but she'd never expected...

"Theresa!" Alex's voice rose. "Look at me. You're in shock right now. I need you to focus. Are you hurt? Can you move?"

The word *shock* snapped her mind back like a jolt to the system. She spent a lot of her professional life explaining to clients that the surreal, frozen feeling people went through in a moment of crisis was perfectly normal. Not that knowing that had prepared her in the slightest for suddenly having her dashing ex come swinging in like an action hero.

"I'm okay. Not hurt." She took a deep breath and let it out slowly.

"Thank You, God." A quick prayer slipped through his lips, then his eyes locked on her face again. "Check him for weapons. Then grab the shotgun. Point it at buddy here. And tell me everything you know about his friends, where they've gone, who this Castor he mentioned is and whatever trunk he thinks I was here to steal. Quickly."

"There were three of them." Quickly she patted down Brick's jacket and the legs. No weapons. Then she pulled the shotgun from a puddle of melting snow and trained it on Brick. Still Alex didn't loosen his grip. "They're looking for a trunk. Castor and Howler left while I was locked in the closet. I don't know where they went. This guy's named Brick. Castor asked me if I knew where Mandy and your sister were. He mentioned Mandy by name."

"Well, as long as Josh is serving overseas we can't ask him what he thinks his second cousin might be mixed up in." Alex's mouth set in a grim line. "Josh's grandfather was in the military, too. Maybe Mandy's side of the family inherited some old war medals or weapons, or something valuable from his tour of duty. Because, for me, a military foot-locker is the first thing that springs to my mind when somebody mentions a trunk. But Mandy's brothers are pretty well-off. Maybe one of them was storing something at their parents' cottage that was worth stealing."

"Maybe," she said. "Castor seemed to think I should know something about it, but I don't. You and Zoe know Josh's family better than I ever did. I wondered if the intended target was Emmett or Kyle, too, not that an old trunk is the usual place a guy who's almost thirty would keep his valuables."

"Did Mandy say anything at all that would shed some light on any of this?" Alex asked.

Theresa shook her head. "No. Mandy was upset, but nothing to make me think she was afraid, let alone of something like this."

"Doesn't mean she wasn't." Alex took a step back, but his grip on Brick's wrist didn't falter.

"Do you have anything to add to this con-versation?" he asked. "How about you tell me what you know about who this Castor is and why he hired you?"

A gun blast shook the air.

"Theresa, get down!" Alex shouted.

She turned toward him. For a second the world froze as she saw the strength that shone in his eyes. Then time sped up again and suddenly it was as if everything was happening at once. Alex dropped Brick's wrist and pulled Theresa to the floor, knocking the couch over in front of them like a shield. A second gun blast sounded, then a third and a fourth, shattering what remained of the windows and tearing up furniture. Brick leaped to his feet, yanked a small handgun from inside his boot and returned fire, momentarily seeming to forget about her and Alex. Only then did she realize she no longer had a grip on the shotgun.

"We can't look for it now," Alex shouted. "Something secure. Somewhere low. Any thoughts?"

"There's a hatch under the floor." She pointed.

They crawled toward the hatch opening. Alex kicked it open. They tumbled through onto the brick floor below. The hatch snapped shut behind them. Darkness filled the space.

Alex urged her up against the very corner of the wall. Then his body covered hers. His heart beat against her back. He pulled a rough tarp over them. Bullets and shotgun blasts rained in the cottage above them, roaring like a hailstorm. Then the noise stopped. Silence surrounded them, punctuated by nothing but the sound of their ragged breaths, their pounding hearts and whispered prayers mingling in the darkness. Her legs cramped beneath her. Her arms were pinned tight against her chest. She started to stretch.

"Wait." Alex's breath filled her ear. "Not yet."

And then she heard the footsteps, one set, walking slowly through the cottage, stepping on the broken glass, kicking furniture aside. There was swearing in a muffled male voice.

Then there was the slow creak of the hatch door opening above them.

Light filtered down through the hole. Fear filled her chest. Panicked prayers filled her heart. Then the hatch clanged shut again, the footsteps moved on and eventually silence fell. After a long moment, Alex unfolded his body and crouched. "Stay here."

He forced the hatch open and looked out.

And she heard him sigh heavily, then pray for God's mercy under his breath.

She crouched up beside him. "Everything okay?"

"I think we're alone. The cottage is a wreck." He hauled his body up through the hole. Then he looked back down at her face. "Brick is dead."

Alex searched the rest of the cottage quickly, while Theresa waited in the relative shelter of the storage hatch. He found nothing. Except for Brick's corpse, they were alone. The cottage had been so totally destroyed it was hard to imagine the criminals having any motive other than causing damage. When he returned to the living room, Theresa had already hauled herself up and was sitting on the edge of the hatch with her legs still dangling in the hole.

Okay, not quite where he'd asked her to wait. But no harm done.

"They're gone, whoever they were." He reached for her hand, helped her up and then closed the hatch behind her. "I only saw one shooter and it was a fleeting glance at that. He was about six-three, I would guess, masked, with square shoulders."

"Sounds like Castor." Her face paled as her gaze ran to where Brick's body now lay. "But that doesn't make sense. Castor knew I was here, too. He should've gone searching for me. But he barely checked the hatch."

"We were pressed right up against the wall in the shadows," Alex said. "If it was Castor, he probably thinks you escaped somehow. Do you have any idea why he would come back just to kill one of his men?"

"I have no idea." She shook her head but she was still looking at Brick's body. "But if it wasn't him, it means somebody else is running around Cedar Lake destroying cottages. This is my fault. I didn't think to check inside his boots when I was looking for weapons, and then I dropped the shotgun. If he'd run instead of returning fire he might not have gotten shot."

Gently, he took her by the shoulders and turned her away from the body.

"Hey, it's not your fault," he said. "You do know that, right? It was chaos. That gun was hidden pretty deep inside his boot. I might've missed it, too. You pointed out the hatch. If we hadn't hidden in there, we might not still be alive, and we can thank God for that."

She nodded and looked down at the ground.

Her lips quivered. He pulled her into his arms and hugged her. She hugged him back. Somehow standing there with their arms around each other felt as instinctively right as breathing.

If someone had told him, even an hour ago, that he would ever hold Theresa in his arms again, he'd have laughed. But he'd loved her once, she'd been his friend and right now she needed him. Something inside him whispered that he wouldn't be able to keep those old, lingering feelings at bay forever, but for right now, he needed to be stronger than his heartache.

"How are you even here?" she asked. "There's no way you could've made the drive that quickly."

"I took a snowmobile across the lake."

"That's crazy." She pulled back out of his embrace. "It's been a really warm winter. Or, at least, it was until recently. The lake never froze properly. There's no way the ice is consistently thick enough for that to be safe, especially in the middle. You could've fallen through."

He crossed his arms. She was right. It hadn't been safe. It had been downright risky.

But her life had been in danger. He'd taken a calculated risk in order to save her.

"It was fine," he said. "I kept an eye on the shifts in the colors of the ice patterns, followed the channel markers and watched out for the buoys. I know this lake." He looked down. "You've got duct tape on your sleeves."

"Castor taped my wrists together behind my back." She ran her hands over her arms self-consciously. "Fortunately, he did it over the sweatshirt and not on my skin."

Part of him wanted to ask if he was right in thinking the sweatshirt was his old one, and if so, why she was wearing it. But something inside stopped him.

"I'm sorry," he said. "How did you get free?"

"I tore it loose on a metal bucket in the cupboard that they threw me in." Her fingers picked at the duct tape. "I'm guessing you haven't heard from Zoe and Mandy?"

His jaw tightened. Surely it couldn't be a coincidence that gunmen decided to ransack Mandy's cottage the same weekend that Zoe brought her up for a quiet study break, could it?

"No," he said. "I tried Zoe's cell phone again before I left the cottage but I couldn't get a signal. I placed a really quick internet call to my boss, Daniel, on the laptop, though, and let him know what was happening. He said he'd keep trying to reach her and obviously that he'd also call the police and send them straight here. But considering the road and the distance, it'll take the police a while to get here and we've got to get out of here, now."

His eyes glanced at the shattered glass of the broken windows.

"Needless to say, we still have a lot we need to talk about," he went on. "But not here. We've got to get somewhere safer and quickly. I don't know who did this, but they could come back, especially if they think you're connected to this secret trunk somehow. Grab your winter gear. I'm going to check out the body."

He could see the desire to argue forming in her eyes. But she pushed it down.

"Okay, we'll talk once we're somewhere safe." She ran for the back hallway.

He crossed over to the body on the floor. He'd always appreciated how focused Theresa could be when necessary. But he desperately wished Zoe hadn't brought Theresa into it. Knowing this whole mess had put her in danger made everything harder. He crouched beside the body on the floor. Brick's winter jacket and gear were a popular, mass-produced brand available from countless stores and told him nothing. He used the camera on his cell phone to take a picture of Brick's face. Then he took the man's wallet from his pocket, flipped it open and pulled out his driver's license.

"Says his name is Kenneth Brick," he called. "He's from Port Hope, Ontario. Age twenty-three. Looks like he works as a cashier at a supermarket."

"Never heard of him, and I've never seen him before."

"Me neither." Alex took a picture of the driver's license, too, put it back in the wallet and set the wallet next to the body. "Should we?"

"One of his buddies said something that made me question if he was familiar with Cedar Lake." She hesitated. "He alluded to an old nickname of mine."

"Well, the kids around here had all sorts of stupid nicknames flying around, none of which were exactly original, so I wouldn't take it personally. But they know who Mandy is, so I wouldn't be surprised if there was some kind of connection to the lake. Let's add that to the list of things we talk about later. Safety first. Talk second."

She didn't look convinced, but they'd paused here long enough and there really wasn't time to draw this conversation out any longer. He grabbed the remains of a blanket and draped it over the body. When he looked up again, Theresa was standing behind him with a backpack in her hand.

He stood up. "What's that?"

"My emergency kit." She slung it over both shoulders. "It's got a first aid kit, a change of clothes, duct tape, a fire starter, a CB radio and some snacks. Everything's in waterproof bags, so it'll be fine in the snow."

He blinked—even though he knew better than to be surprised, considering it was Theresa. He waited as she slid a pair of snow pants on over her jeans and laced up a pair of winter boots. Then she pulled a heavy, hooded winter jacket on and zipped it up.

They ran for the back door and pushed out into the snow. It was already up to their calves and growing deeper by the second. She followed him down the driveway and into a small, wooden storage shed.

"The snow's gotten bad." Theresa shook the flakes from her hair.

"It's going to get a lot worse," Alex said. What had fallen so far was only a small taste of the deluge the forecast was predicting. He took the spare helmet off the back of the snowmobile and gave it to her. "My truck is back at my cottage. So, the plan is we head to my cottage, I'll call Daniel with my laptop, fill him in and we'll figure out our next move. Hopefully the power will still be on when we get there and Zoe will be sitting there with Mandy, waiting for us."

He closed his eyes. *Lord, I just pray that wherever Zoe is, she's all right. She's strong and she's fierce. But she might be out in a snowstorm with a client I'm not sure I trust and killers on the loose.*

When he opened his eyes, Theresa was looking at him. Strands of dark hair had slipped from the furry hood of her ski jacket. Even now, in the gloomy light of the shed, with flakes swirling like a meteor shower behind her, he had to admit he'd never seen anything like her. It was hard to put into words, but in a world of unstable and transient things, Theresa had always been like a tree, a willow tree, maybe, with roots so long and deep he knew if he just stayed close enough to her he could ride out any storm.

Until she'd cut him off, and left him rootless and drifting.

"I know you're worried about Zoe." Theresa's hand brushed his arm. "She's going to be okay. She's smart. If she made it to town and saw the weather forecast before the storm hit, she probably just found a coffee shop or restaurant to ride it out in."

"I hope so." He waited as she put the helmet on then climbed on the snowmobile. Her long legs slid over the back of it behind him. She hesitated. Then her hands slid about his waist, in a gesture somehow both so familiar and foreign that he felt his brain almost short-circuit for a moment as he reached for the ignition. "Hold tight. This could get rough."

The engine turned over.

A tall, broad-shouldered figure in a ski mask stepped into the open doorway, blocking their way to freedom. There was a small, automatic handgun in his hand. "You two aren't going anywhere."

THREE

Fear washed over Theresa's body. Instinctively her arms tightened around Alex's body.

It was Castor. It had to be. His dark, masked form stood silhouetted against the snow. But the voice and stance were unmistakable. The head of the gang of kidnappers and killers who'd raided the cottage was back, filling the doorway and blocking their escape.

"I said, get off the snowmobile!" He stretched his arm out to its full length and tilted the gun sideways, like some kind of television gangster. "Both of you. Now. With your hands up."

There was no way past him. They were stuck in a tiny little shed and he was about to shoot them at point-blank range. Her limbs began to shake. Her grip loosened on Alex's body. Tears choked in the back of her throat and mingled with prayer.

Alex gunned the engine.

The snowmobile shot forward. Her body bounced back hard against the seat. The weapon fired. The snowmobile swerved hard to the right and she clung to Alex so tightly her arms ached. A second bullet split the air. Then she felt wind and snow smacking her body again. She opened her eyes. The snowmobile was flying through the woods. Bullets echoed behind them in the trees. Then the sound faded and all she could hear was the rush of the engine beneath her and the beating of her own heart in her chest. Trees grew thick around them, pressing in on all sides. Jagged rocks seemed to burst through the snow. Flakes filled her eyes like they were shooting through a galaxy of stars. She held on.

What was he thinking driving straight at Castor like that? Yes, Alex had saved their lives. Again. But he'd done so by risking getting shot. Something about that made her feel almost indignant. Alex was the kind of guy who'd just free-fall through life, trusting things would work out okay. Sure, he was right most of the time. In fact, there wasn't a doubt in her mind that she was safer on the back of Alex's snowmobile than she would be with anyone else in the world driving at this kind of speed, through these woods, in the snow. But did that mean he had what it took to be anybody's bodyguard? Who'd pick up the pieces if, the next time he launched himself into danger, he was wrong?

As a teenager, the strong, daring young man with sun-bleached hair and dazzling blue eyes had always seemed like something out of a teenage heartthrob fantasy. She'd had a girlhood crush on him long before the day he'd dashingly rescued her from the capsized sailboat. Wakeboarding, water skiing, diving off the cliffs—it had seemed like there was nothing he couldn't do. Except plan or think for more than two seconds ahead. There was a world of difference between instinctively leaping into action to rescue someone from a capsized boat and impulsively dropping out of college. She hadn't been sure back then that Alex knew the difference. She'd lost count of how many times Zoe had recently tried to convince her that Alex had grown up and wasn't that reckless guy anymore. Maybe. But she had yet to see it.

God, forgive me for sounding ungrateful. I'm thankful that Alex rescued me. Thank You that we both got out of there alive. But please, help him be wise and actually think through what we're going to do next, to find Zoe and Mandy, and get us all home safe and alive.

The snowmobile was slowing already. She sat back. They'd left the Rhodes family cottage only a few minutes ago, but now another building loomed ahead of them out of the snow. A moment later she recognized the shape. It was Number Seven Cedar Lake, the Pattersons' cottage. Despite the size of the lake, its wild and rugged landscape meant there were only eleven cottages dotted around it, like the numbers on a misshapen clock. They were owned by five different extended families, now that her family had sold their cottage: the Rhodes, the Deans, the Pattersons, the Mullocks and the Wrights.

John and Judith Patterson were a sweet, elderly couple who spent their summers at their small, nonwinterized cottage and every winter at their condo in Florida. Their son, Don, was a widower who'd built a large A-frame for himself and his children, Natalie and Corey, after his wife had died tragically. It had probably been twenty years ago now, and she'd been just a kid at the time, but still she remembered how everyone came together to help.

Then Don had been the first one to leap

to her parents' aid, years later, when they'd lost their business, buying up what remained of their inventory and taking over the lease on their store for his lumber business. Sudden sadness filled her chest so sharply it hurt. The little Cedar Lake community had been like a second, extended family who looked out for one another. One that she'd lost the summer she'd lost Alex.

The snowmobile slid smoothly around the far side of the cottage under the side awning. Alex cut the motor and they sat there for a half a breath, hearing nothing but the wind shaking the trees and snow buffeting the awning above them. Then, slowly, she pulled her arms from around his waist. He slid his visor up and looked back over his shoulder. "Are you okay?"

The depth of genuine concern in his tone was probably the only thing that kept her from asking if he had any idea what he was doing. At least now they'd have a moment to regroup.

She slid her visor up, too. "Yes, I'm okay. That man in the mask was Castor. I'm pretty sure of it."

"Well, I think he's the same man I saw shooting up the Rhodeses's cottage and who killed Brick. Which does not bode well." Alex swung his leg over and stood up. "Can I take it from the look on your face that you don't like something about how I handled things back there?"

Was she still that transparent around him?

"You drove a snowmobile straight at a gunman."

"He was going to kill us. We may not know much about these guys, but we know they're not above murder." He stretched. "But they're also sloppy and reckless. Castor, as you call him, was only holding the gun with one hand. Which is cute if you're trying to look all tough, but absolute garbage when it comes to aiming. My gut told me that if I was fast enough off the mark he'd have no hope of hitting us." He shrugged. "I was right."

All right, he had been right about that. Her studies in human psychology told her that there was a lot to be said for reading body language like that, and she could even concede that sometimes a person's instincts took over and acted, before the rational brain had processed what they already knew. But it was one thing to believe these men were nothing but a ragtag group of amateurs. It was another to risk your life on that.

"So, we've stopped here to talk things

through and make a plan?" She climbed off, too. The fact that Castor had killed his own henchman worried her, as did the fact he hadn't taken the time to thoroughly check every corner of the cottage when he'd found her gone—despite how relieved she was he hadn't seen them. But for now, she could only guess what all that could mean.

"Pretty much," Alex said. "We should be safe here for a bit. This cottage is pretty hard to find from the main lake road if you don't know what you're looking for. If they were coming after us on snowmobiles we should have heard them by now. I'm going to try to call Zoe again on my cell phone and, also, the police and Daniel. Not that I expect I'll be able to get a signal. So I'd like to try the CB radio, too. But that's going to be trickier because anything we say on an open channel could be overheard."

"Absolutely." Theresa eased the backpack off her shoulders and pulled out the radio. "I'm sorry. You must be worried sick."

"Yeah, I am." He took it from her. "Zoe's not just my little sister. She's my colleague, and right now she's somewhere with our client."

He strode off down the side of the cottage under the porch roof.

"Alex, wait! You said you're worried about being overheard on the radio. Like I tried to tell you, one of the guys called me by an old nickname." She took a deep breath. "In fact, it was 'finicky little princess.'"

She didn't know what kind of response she'd expected from that, but it wasn't the one she got. He didn't even turn. "Okay, well, we can talk about that after if you think that means anything."

If it meant anything? Didn't he remember?

"But the kids at Cedar Lake used to call me princess, remember? And they thought I was spoiled."

He still didn't turn.

"The only person who ever called me a 'finicky little princess' was you. Just you. When you broke off our engagement."

Alex spun back. His face had gone oddly pale. He opened his mouth, and for a long moment no words came out.

"I don't know what I'm supposed to say to that," he managed, finally. "I'm sorry if whatever those thugs said reminded you of our breakup. I don't remember things like you apparently do. Certainly, I never meant to hurt you. But right now, our past doesn't matter."

She could tell he was upset, but she didn't

know why. Did it bother him to be reminded that he was the one who'd broken off their engagement? Either way he was completely failing to get what she was saying. Like when he'd seemed to think "I don't know if I can marry you right now" had meant "Please go away forever. I don't love you anymore."

"Listen," she said. "Please. What I'm saying is that it was very bizarre and specific. Added to the fact he seemed convinced I knew something about this trunk, which I don't, it makes me think that maybe he had some kind of deeper link to our history here."

"Maybe? I don't know. It sounds like a pretty big leap of logic to me." He didn't look convinced. "But we can talk about it more when I've located Zoe and Mandy, we're somewhere safe, we're not trying to outrun a pending storm and nobody's shooting at us. Just give me half a second and then we'll keep going. Won't be long."

He turned away. She nearly groaned. The storm was growing worse by the second. His sister and Mandy were missing. She'd just been kidnapped and shot at. A man was dead. Yet here they were, reliving the very same kind of argument they'd had a hundred times before. He wanted to leap into action.

She wanted to pause long enough to actually think.

Alex had already given up on the cell phone and was fiddling with the radio. She glanced at the cottage. The families at Cedar Lake used to have an open-door policy for all the kids on the lake in case of emergency. Maybe she could still find a key. Her hand ran along the underside of the window boxes, feeling in the snow. Then she stopped short. The cottage door was already ajar.

"Hey, Alex? I think the cottage is open."

No response. She pressed her hand against the door. It swung open under her touch.

She stepped inside the cottage and cried out in shock.

It had been ransacked.

Theresa's cry was faint and yet to Alex's ears it seemed to rise above the sound of the wind and the static hissing in his ear.

"Theresa?" He turned back. For a moment he couldn't see her, just snow swirling around the empty place he'd left her standing just moments ago. He ran back three strides and burst through the open door. The cottage had been turned inside out. Drawers hung open. Furniture was tossed. They'd theorized the carnage at the Rhodeses' cottage had had something to do with Josh's second cousins and maybe something expensive one of them owned. But why ransack a neighboring cottage? Theresa stood in the clutter. Her hand rose to her lips.

"The poor Pattersons," she said.

He slid his helmet off. Theresa still had her back to him. His hand reached up instinctively to slide around her shoulder. At the last moment, he caught himself and brought his hand back down, just before his fingertips brushed the back of her neck. He set the helmet down and slid his hands into his pockets.

"We knew Castor and his buddies were looking for a trunk," he said. "Maybe they're going door to door looking for it."

"Mandy's brothers have done well for themselves financially, and Castor mentioned her by name. So I could at least come up with some theories why somebody would rob them. But the Pattersons are just a really nice, low-key, modest family who never did anything to anyone…" Then she turned back suddenly and he could see the same question crossing her mind that had just crossed his.

"Except for Corey," he finished.

Corey Patterson was four years younger than Alex and had gotten in trouble with the law for drug possession at sixteen. Alex wasn't sure of all the details. But sometime around the time they'd been getting engaged, Josh's dad, who was a cop, had smelled marijuana on Corey and threatened to turn him in. Rumor had it that Corey had been in trouble with the law off and on after that. Then, around the time their engagement had ended, Corey had been charged with possession.

"Whatever happened to him?" Theresa leaned against the wall.

"I honestly don't know," Alex said. "I kind of checked out of what was going on up here after you and I broke up. Last I heard, he'd been sent to a youth rehabilitation facility. All my mom would say is that every family had their problems. I just can't imagine anyone doing this to their own grandparents. I hate to say this, but if they're ransacking small cottages then they probably hit your family's cottage, too."

"My family doesn't have a cottage here anymore. I thought you knew that." She crossed over to where a jumble of smashed pictures in frames littered the floor. "They sold it years ago to pay off their business debts."

She said it so calmly. Like she was pointing out the color of the sky or the existence of dirt on the ground. Like it was a given and he should know. But he hadn't. And that irked him.

"No, I didn't know," he said. He watched as she bent down and carefully brushed the glass out of a broken frame. "I had absolutely no idea. How's the business doing now?"

"It's gone, too. They sold it at a loss." Now there really was a hint of reproach in her voice. "A long time ago. Remember there was a big fire shortly after we got engaged? Well, when they lost the battle with the insurance company they were forced to sell the business, the cottage, our house—all of it—to settle their debts."

What? His mind spun. His sister, his family and Josh all had to have known about this. Had he been so determined to shut down any conversation about Theresa that they'd never brought it up with him? Or, worse, had they presumed he'd already known?

"There was a huge auction." She stood up slowly, the picture still in her fingers. "You must know this."

"Well, I honestly didn't." Heat rose to the back of his neck. His voice sounded louder than he'd meant it to. While he'd been on the video call with Theresa he'd wondered why

Zoe hadn't relocated them to the Vaughans' cottage at the mouth of the lake. He'd never imagined the Vaughans no longer owned it. "When exactly was all this?"

"The end of the summer we were supposed to get married. I told you, my parents were having problems—"

"Money problems. Not 'losing everything' problems—"

The lines around her mouth set hard, like she was biting something back.

"Well, at the time we broke up it wasn't public knowledge," she said. "They put the cottage up for sale at the end of that summer and held an auction for the furniture and the stock left in the store that the creditors didn't take back. Don Patterson took over the lease of the actual store building for his business. But sadly it wasn't enough to keep them from losing the house. The whole thing was a slow, painful death that took a very long time."

He ran his hand slowly over his jaw. "I'm sorry."

The words seemed so inadequate, but he didn't know what else to say.

"Thanks. It was a long time ago. Now, can you do me a favor and take a cell phone picture of this?" She bent down and picked up a glossy photograph in a broken frame, changing the topic before he could press any further. "It would feel wrong to take it with me, but I think it might be helpful to have while we're trying to figure out what's happening here."

She held it up and for the first time he saw what she'd rescued from the glass. It was a group picture of the Cedar Lake barbecue, taken the summer he was twenty. Almost fifty people between the ages of two and eighty clustered around the warm rocks that jutted out into the lake in front of the Vaughan's family cottage. Half of them were kids or teens, many of whom had been his friends. He was sitting off to the side in a huge wooden Adirondack chair. He, Theresa, Zoe and Josh had won the Cedar Lake scavenger hunt for the very first time that year, beating out the stronger group of Emmett, Kyle and their friend Paul Wright.

The gold, spray-painted coffee mug that served as a trophy was clutched in Alex's left hand. Nineteen-year-old Theresa sat on the arm of his chair, her back leaning against his shoulder. The sun soaked her long tanned limbs. Her head was tossed back, caught mid-laugh, no doubt at whatever he'd been whispering in her ear, which, judging by the grin on his face, he'd thought was pretty funny.

A huge diamond dazzled on her finger. He'd proposed to her that day, on the edge of the rock in front of her cottage, while they'd been out together scavenging for whatever treasures had been hidden in the woods. The ring was even bigger than he remembered. It'd been so far beyond what he was able to afford that Theresa's father had pulled him aside later that night to ask how he was going to pay for it.

He could still remember the moment that picture was taken. He'd never been happier than he'd been the moment she'd said yes. He'd never wanted anything in life as much as he'd wanted to marry her. His eyes slid from the cell phone camera up to Theresa's face, as years' worth of words he never got to say suddenly smacked inside him like a tidal wave.

Lord, what happened to us? How did something so amazing get so destroyed?

He swallowed hard. "Look, Theresa, I—"

"Break, break." A child's voice buzzed from the CB radio on his belt, and it was only then he realized the channel was open. "Bee to Hive. Come in Hive."

Was there another family up at Cedar Lake?

He yanked the radio from his belt and raised it to his mouth. "Hey, kid. I don't what you're doing on this line. But a radio isn't a toy, especially not with a storm coming. Where are your parents? Because if you're in a cottage right now they should really pack up and head for town."

There was a pause. Then the child said, "Copy. Negative. I'm in a house. I'm not at a cottage and you're rude. Over and out."

The line went dead.

"In my experience, little kids hate being spoken to like little kids," Theresa said mildly.

"I was worried his family might be up at a cottage around here and not know about the weather situation," he said. "But it seems your radio's getting a decent range. There are any number of houses on the highway that boy might be in. But I don't know what his parents were thinking, letting him play with a CB radio."

"It was a girl. I'm guessing somewhere between the ages of eight and ten." A slight smile turned up the corners of her lips. "And we used to play on CB radios when we kids all the time. Remember? Paul Wright's father was a trucker and got us all hooked. We used them during the scavenger hunt. Or whenever you wanted to talk to me late at night without risking my parents answering the cottage phone."

True. He hadn't gotten a cell phone until he was eighteen and cell service at the lake had always been nonexistent. Life had been one big adventure back then: slipping through the woods, hiding together from the other scavenger hunt teams and whispering coded messages to her over a walkie-talkie, as if how they felt about each other was a secret they needed to protect from the world.

The ironic thing was that now he was living the kind of life he'd only played at back then. Stopping evil and protecting people from danger was no longer just some unattainable dream. It was his job and his calling. But did Theresa even see who he'd become? Or did she still think he was some reckless boy running through the trees playing at being a hero?

He set the radio down on the table, fished his useless cell phone out of his pocket and took a picture of the group photo.

"Kenneth Brick was obviously using his last name as a nickname," Theresa said. "But that doesn't mean Howler and Castor are. One or both of them could be someone we know using a nickname to hide their identity."

He nodded. "Agreed."

"If Kenneth Brick is twenty-three, then he'd have been about fourteen around the time this picture was taken, right?" Theresa asked. "If we assume that Howler and Castor are in their twenties, too, and that one of them is in this picture, then we're looking at anybody in the picture between the age of, say, eleven and twenty."

He scanned the picture. He spotted Mandy quickly. She was eleven back then and sitting cross-legged in the sun between her older brothers. There were ten people in the picture who'd be in their twenties now. Six he dismissed immediately. Theresa, Zoe, Josh and Alex himself could be struck off the list. So could Mandy's twin brothers, Emmett and Kyle, not just because they were slightly too old, but because it was hard to imagine the owner of a successful car dealership or a local politician hiring somebody to ransack their parents' cottage. But, still, he couldn't discount the possibility one of them was Castor's target.

That left just four people.

"Natalie Patterson, Corey Patterson, Tanner Mullock and Paul Wright," he said.

"Paul would be about twenty-seven now,"

Theresa said. "I don't know where he is, but I know he was always big into hunting and won the scavenger hunt with the Rhodes twins every year, until we finally took the trophy. All I know about Tanner Mullock is that he came up to the lake to stay with his grandparents a couple of summers because his parents were going through marriage problems. He's probably in his midtwenties now. There wasn't a woman on the crew, so Natalie's out. Although we can't dismiss the possibility she could be romantically linked to Castor or someone on his crew."

"Which leaves just Corey as the only one we knew who got in trouble with the law," Alex said. As wonderful as theories were, they were getting nowhere. "What we need to do right now is focus on finding Zoe and Mandy, and for that I need a phone signal. Hopefully the police are on their way and we just haven't crossed paths with them yet."

The CB buzzed again with that odd whine of a signal flickering in and out. He reached for it but Theresa got to it first.

"Let me talk to the girl," Theresa said. "You're right, she's probably nowhere near Cedar Lake. But I might be able to talk to her parents, who could to put a call through to the police to back up the last report, as well as calling Zoe and Daniel."

"Not a bad idea, but she's just a kid playing around with a radio. Plus, she hung up on me."

"I'm used to talking to kids." Theresa held it up to her mouth. Her fingers lightly brushed the dials bringing the signal in stronger. "Break, break. Calling Bee. Come in, Bee."

There was a hiss of static. Then a deep voice, with a hint of cruel laughter floated down the line.

"Well, hello, princess." It was Castor. "Isn't this a nice surprise? You must be pretty pleased with yourself pulling an escape like that. How long do you think you'll be able to hide from me?"

Theresa's shoulders straightened. Defiance gleamed in her eyes. "You're a murderer and a thug. But you haven't found that trunk you're looking for yet, have you? Otherwise you wouldn't be taunting us."

"Listen here," Castor spluttered. "You're nothing but a spoiled, entitled little snob who deserves what's coming to her. But I'm going to find that trunk, and then I'm going to find you and kill you. Because I've found your friend Zoe Dean. After that car accident, I was the one who riddled the car with bullet holes, while she ran away like a coward."

What was he talking about? Alex's brain swam. What accident? Why would Zoe be alone in the car without Mandy?

"I found Zoe and dragged her back to the Rhodeses' cottage screaming and crying for mercy!" Castor spat out the words with so much venom he was almost shouting. "I've got her here with me, right now, kneeling on the floor with a gun pointed to her head. So, here's what's going to happen. You're going to come back here and start thinking really hard about where you might've seen that trunk, otherwise I'm going to kill her."

Anger burned like fire through Alex's veins. "No, you listen to me! You're not going to lay a hand on my sister. You're going to let her go. Because I'm on my way over there—"

But the words froze on his tongue as the CB went dead.

FOUR

Static hissed through the CB radio. A cry of frustration left Alex's lungs that was so strong and filled with pain it was almost primal. He grabbed the radio from Theresa's hand.

"Hello? Hello?" There was no one there. Castor was gone. He was going to kill Zoe. Alex couldn't let that happen.

"I've got to go." He grabbed his snowmobile helmet and turned the radio's volume down, until the whining rise and fall of the static wasn't much more than a whisper. "I've got no choice. I'm going to go back to the Rhodeses' cottage and confront Castor. Hopefully, Zoe will still be alive when I get there." He couldn't let himself think otherwise. "I don't know what I'm going to do. But I'll come up with something on the way. I can't let those monsters hurt my sister."

"Alex, stop—"

"No, you stop. We can't afford to just sit around and talk about this right now. My sister is in danger. Some killer has her, and he's going to hurt her if I don't get there and stop him."

"But you don't understand. He didn't hang up on you—"

"Yes, he did."

"Just stop for a moment and let me explain—"

"What would've happened to you, an hour ago, if I'd stopped instead of racing across the ice to rescue you? Or when your sailboat capsized when we were teenagers if I hadn't jumped in to save you?" He felt her hand brush his arm. But he pulled away and started down the narrow front hallway. "Hide. Find a safe space in here somewhere, make yourself as small as you can, and don't come out again until I come for you, okay? You should be safe here. There's no reason to believe they'd come back here. Just stay hidden and don't come out."

"Alex!" Her voice rose. "You're not listening."

"I don't have time to stop and talk." He strode toward the door. He heard her feet behind him. Then suddenly she hugged him from behind, hard, with arms wrapped tight around his shoulders, just like she had back when they cared about each other and he'd been about to run off somewhere without remembering to say goodbye. "Theresa, don't. You know I can just shrug you off and keep going."

"I know." Her breath came hard and fast in his ear. "But the Alex I knew never would."

"Don't do this to me," he said. "Don't make me choose between standing here talking to you and going to save my sister."

"I don't think he has Zoe. I'm almost positive he doesn't." Her arms slid off his body. "Also he didn't hang up on us. I hung up on him."

"You did what?" He turned toward her. "That wasn't your call to make!"

Frustration, confusion, anger and fear all battled inside him like rising bubbles in a boiling pot and for a moment his voice could barely rise above a whisper. She stepped back. And for a moment, the depth of pain and fear echoing in her eyes, mirroring his own feelings right back at him, seemed to be the only thing that kept him grounded. "How could you do that to me?"

"He was lying to us." Theresa leaned

against the wall and dropped down to sit, as if her legs no longer had the strength to hold her. "He doesn't have Zoe. He just doesn't."

He stood there for a moment, looking down at her, not even knowing what to feel.

Theresa folded her legs beneath her and sat cross-legged, with her elbows on her knees and her head in her hands. "I didn't trust what he was saying, so I just changed the channel for a second, to make it look like we'd lost the signal, so he wouldn't realize we were stalling for time. I thought it would throw him off and grab us a quick few seconds to talk. You were running hot. I never expected he'd just give up and disappear altogether." Her eyes were locked on a patch of floor by her feet. "He's lying through his teeth. If you leave here and go back to Mandy's family cottage, you won't find Zoe there. Trust me. It's a trap."

Thoughts and feelings were still flying through his mind so rapidly he couldn't even figure out how to put any of them into words. His legs practically burned with the drive to bolt out the door to the snowmobile. But Zoe trusted Theresa's impressions of people. So did Daniel and Josh. And a long time ago, so did he. He set his helmet down on the floor and sat down opposite her. "How could you possibly know that?"

"There are a dozen little things you can pick up about how people's voices change when they're not telling the truth. It was partly the inflection in his voice and partly the words he said. He didn't sound confident. He didn't sound like a man who knew he had the advantage, let alone something of major value to bargain with. He sounded like a panicked fool who was getting desperate."

Zoe had always said it was like Theresa had a built-in lie detector, which was part of what'd made her such a valuable ally and asset. Still, she'd just cut off a criminal who claimed he was going to kill Alex's sister.

"I'm listening. Convince me."

"He didn't once mention Mandy." She looked up at him. "I can't imagine Zoe leaving her alone, can you? He made it sound like Zoe had run away from some car crash, like a coward, and that he had to drag her back, begging and crying. Does any of that sound anything like the Zoe you know?"

"No. No it doesn't." He leaned his head back against the wall. If anything, it sounded like the exact opposite of Zoe. "But just because he was lying about that doesn't mean he was lying about everything. And you were still wrong to cut him off like that."

"Did you even hear what you were saying to him? You were emotional. You were seconds away from tipping them off to exactly how far away we were."

Heat rose to the back of his neck. Because while he was certain that wasn't true, Theresa had clearly thought it was. "Just how foolish do you think I am?"

"I never said I thought you were foolish." She sounded a lot calmer than he felt. "I thought you were impulsive. You were running hot. You still are. Barely an hour ago, you risked your life and leaped onto a snowmobile with no weapons, no backup and no plan and just dashed across the frozen lake—"

"To save your life!" His voice rose.

"You risked your life!" Her voice rose to match his.

"Yeah! Because you really mattered to me! I couldn't stand the idea of you getting hurt!" His voice filled in the narrow hallway and bounced back to his ears. Theresa gasped and, as he watched, something softened behind her eyes. For the first time in a long time, he felt the impulse to just reach out and hold her hand. His voice dropped. "So, yeah, I was willing to risk my life for you. Twice. Just like I'd risk it now to save my sister."

It was as if the hallway were shrinking and the walls pushing them closer toward each other. Static buzzed quietly from the walkie-talkie. He could hear the sound of his own heart pounding.

"Well, people care about you, too, and don't want you dying for them." Her voice was barely above a whisper. Her eyes met his for a long moment. Then she looked away. "Anyway, like I said, I had no idea he was just going to disappear like that. I thought they'd hear static long enough for us to talk but not long enough to get suspicious. Then we could come back to them with something more planned and measured."

He could understand that. She'd made a call based on what she thought was the right thing to do and it just hadn't worked out. But still, the fact she'd done it at all, because she thought they were apparently some kind of team, and that he was about to get them into danger, made it even harder to swallow. As far as he was concerned the dynamic was pretty simple. She was in trouble. He was saving her. But that didn't mean he couldn't use her advice.

"Okay, then, in your professional opinion, what do you think it means that Castor hung up?" he asked.

She paused for a very long moment. Then she said, "Castor's being impulsive. He's being reckless and seems to have no real plan in mind. He took the risk of making up a big lie on the spot, counting on the fact we still didn't know where Zoe and Mandy were. When that didn't work, he stopped trying instead of doubling down. I definitely think that if he'd really had Zoe and wanted to barter for her life, he'd have tried contacting us again by now, with an even bigger threat. He'd have almost definitely put her voice on the line to punish you and prove he wasn't lying. He wouldn't have just given up. Then again, randomly shooting up the Rhodeses' cottage makes no sense, either. We're dealing with somebody desperate. Somebody who doesn't seem to be thinking consistently. Not a criminal mastermind."

Not that it made them any safer.

"He was unbelievably rude to you." Alex shook his head. "I figured he was just making up nasty things to taunt you. But you think he was trying to lure us out because it's possible he thinks you know something about the trunk?"

"If so, I have no idea what it would be," she said. "If I did know anything about the trunk, it was so long ago I've forgotten."

"Do you honestly believe there's some valuable treasure in a trunk, hidden somewhere in a cottage at Cedar Lake?"

"No," she said. "Not really. But I'm not sure if it even matters. All that matters is that Castor and Howler think there is and are willing to kill for it."

He leaned his head back and looked up at the ceiling. "What could they possibly think is in some old trunk that's worth killing for?" he asked.

"People kill for all sorts of reasons—desperation, fear, love, jealousy, hate." Even without looking at her, he could tell she was shrugging. "Some people would kill for a hundred dollars. Some people wouldn't kill for a million."

He closed his eyes and prayed for wisdom. What were his options? He could leave Theresa here and go back to the Rhodeses' cottage. But if Theresa was right, he was walking into a trap for no good reason, all the while leaving her here alone, unprotected. He could head back to the Rhodeses' and take Theresa with him, which could mean leading them both into a trap.

Help me, Lord. I thought I had the skills and training for this. But I never counted on the woman I used to care about being in the mix.

"Okay, I've made a decision," he said. "We're going to keep going around the lake to my cottage. Once we're there, we'll grab my truck and head out of here. I'll leave you somewhere safe, like a coffee shop or motel, and then head back to find Zoe and Mandy. But I'm still hoping, despite our very remote location and the horrible weather, we will still manage to run into the police and they'll take care of you from there."

Everything would be easier once he no longer had Theresa to worry about. What he did after that still remained to be seen.

He stood up then reached down for Theresa's hand. She unfolded slowly.

"One more thing." Her nose wrinkled. She took his hand and let him help her up. "That lie Castor told about there being a car accident was oddly specific. I don't know for sure, but part of me thinks he was talking about it as if it was a real event that he thought we already knew had happened."

Something twisted painfully in his chest. "Which means?"

Fear flickered in her eyes. "Which I think means we should be prepared for the possibility Zoe, or somebody else, was in a car accident."

They closed the door to the Pattersons' cottage behind them as best they could, then stood for a moment under the limited shelter of the awning and listened.

"For what it's worth, I'm confident that Zoe would've seen how bad the weather is and just stayed in town," Theresa said, sliding her helmet over her head. "She wouldn't have had any reason to worry that I would be in danger."

His gloved hand touched hers briefly. "I hope so."

The sky hung low and pale gray above them as they drove. The snow had stopped falling, which he knew was just the lull before the storm. At least another inch and a half of snow had fallen since he'd left the Rhodeses' cottage and if the weather forecast was right, at least ten times that was going to fall before the day was through. He could feel Theresa's arms around his waist. She shivered against him, and he almost smiled. She'd never liked the winter as much as he did. Some of the other kids at the lake had teased her about that, too, and called her thin-skinned. Looking back, it was amazing how much teasing she'd taken, all for being beautiful and having a few nice things. But from the perspective of a love-struck young man, it was as if she'd been so full of inner light that she came alive when the rays of sunshine soaked into her skin.

Guilt about her family situation stirred something inside him. Had she told him? Had she tried to tell him and he hadn't listened? They'd both been so young. Maybe they'd had no business making that kind of commitment. When he'd seen that dazzling ring in the jewelry store window, he'd actually gone, gotten a credit card and maxed it out to pay for the most expensive ring he could find, only to later have her father gently point out to him privately that that had been an incredibly unwise first step in preparing to be married.

Truth was, he'd had no clue what he was going to do with his life back then. Now, here he was, all these years later, just three months into the official launch of Ash Private Security, finally starting the career he felt like he'd been created for.

The cottage road was uneven and turned sharply as it dipped and curled around Cedar Lake. They crested a hill and a fork in the road spread out beneath them. To his right the road continued around the mouth of the lake, passing the cottage that once belonged to Theresa's family on the route back to his family's place, where he'd parked the truck.

Straight ahead lay the road away from the lake leading to the highway. His mind spun quickly. Mandy's brother Emmett had recently bought a dilapidated house on an offshoot of the lake, near the highway. Alex and Zoe had agreed that if disaster struck they'd meet there. It didn't have power and wasn't the kind of place a person could comfortably camp out for long. But he could drop Theresa off there in safety and then continue up the highway until he got a cell phone signal. He wouldn't be leaving her for long and he would definitely be more likely to get a signal faster that way. He might even be able to flag somebody down to help.

He gritted his teeth, made a judgment call and drove straight. He could feel Theresa tap-

ping him on the shoulder, no doubt wanting
to ask him what they were doing. He didn't
slow. They'd done a whole lot of talking back
at the Pattersons' and now it was time to just
make a decision and go with it. The truck was
safer. But just staying on the snowmobile and
not going back for it would be faster. Despite
Theresa's reassurances, Castor's cruel words
still twisted in the back of his mind. Zoe was
his sister and his colleague. Mandy was their
client. Theresa was an unfortunate casualty
of all this. The sooner he got her out of danger and found somewhere safe to leave her,
the quicker he'd be able to find them.

The road grew narrower, cutting between a
steep incline leading down to the lake on one
side and forest rising on the other. Winding
turns sent their bodies rising up off the seat
and back down hard again. He knew this road
like he knew his skin. Just twenty more minutes and Cedar Lake would be behind them.
He breached another hill, already mentally
preparing for the next turn, where he knew
the road took a sharp, steep turn to the left.

The hairpin turn loomed. His heart stopped.
A mess of desperately swerving tire tracks
and broken branches covered the road ahead
of them. A vehicle of some sort had careened

down the hill ahead, lost control and failed to make the turn. Theresa squeezed his shoulder hard. His eyes scanned the broken trees on the right, looking down the steep drop to the lake, hoping with each breath to find some evidence to counter the picture that was forming.

But between the devastation and the tire tracks, the story was clear. A vehicle had slid off this road, crashed through the trees and plummeted down the hill toward the frozen water.

The snowmobile slid to a stop. Before Theresa could react, Alex leaped off and pelted down the road toward the broken trees. She pulled her helmet off and ran after him. Was it Zoe's car that had left the road and split the trees? Frozen tears rose to her eyes as prayers she could barely find words for swirled through her heart like scattered snowflakes. Castor had been telling the truth about there having been a car accident. The fact she'd suspected that did nothing to temper the shock of seeing the violent devastation the crash had caused.

If he'd been telling the truth about Zoe, she'd never forgive herself.

Lord, please have mercy on the victims of

this crash. I had no idea it could be something this bad. Please, may Zoe and Mandy still be safe and alive.

Alex reached the spot where the tire tracks disappeared. He scrambled over the side of the road and started climbing down the steep, slippery incline through the trees. Through the bracken and snow she could barely see the front wheels of an overturned vehicle. The car had completely flipped.

"Stay back." Alex raised a gloved hand in her direction. "It's really not safe."

She stopped, her boots at the edge of the road, watching as he half climbed and half slid his way toward the car. The ground below was an obstacle course of snow-covered shapes, strewn with broken glass and car debris. He scrambled over a rock and disappeared from view. Her hand grabbed onto a pine tree. She'd been called to traffic accidents before. She could handle this. She braced herself and eyed the ground, and took a sideways step. "I'm coming down. I can help."

"No, please don't!" Alex's face appeared between the trees. "Stay on the road. It's incredibly slippery and dangerous. It's almost a straight drop below me. I'll holler if I find anyone who needs help. But it's not Zoe's car."

Relief filled her lungs with a deep gasp of icy air. Alex carefully made his way around a tree that seemed to be growing almost horizontally from the hill below her. He disappeared from sight again.

"The car is sort of dangling partway down the hill." Alex's voice wafted up from below her. "It seems to be wedged upside down between two trees and a giant rock. But the ground's so steep down here I can barely stand. I'm afraid if I'm not careful, I'll send it rolling down the hill into the lake. I don't know about you, but I really don't feel like crashing through the ice today."

He was trying to make a joke. He did that when he was stressed. She didn't much feel like smiling.

"And you're sure it's not Zoe's car?" she asked.

"One hundred percent," he said. "Trust me. I have no idea whose car this is. But even upside down I can tell it's a zippy little red sports car without snow tires. They didn't have a hope of navigating safely in this kind of weather." His voice disappeared again. Then she heard an odd, muffled grunt, like he'd barely managed to stop himself from shouting out in surprise. Then he was back. "Just give me a minute, okay? I need to focus and that means we can't keep yapping."

She stepped back from the ledge. That was the closest he'd even come to being sharp with her. When they'd been younger, he'd been so laid-back about everything it had driven her crazy. He'd floated through life like a kite on the wind. While for her, life had always felt more like digging deep, like a shovel in the dirt—even before her parents' financial troubles. But now there was something different in Alex's tone. In fact, there had been ever since he'd challenged Brick. Now his voice sounded more as if he'd given up coasting for blasting charges through the rock.

Alex seemed harder than he used to be, both inside and out. She wasn't sure what to make of it.

She waited a long moment, listening to the trees sway and the muffled sounds of Alex struggling to do something far below where she couldn't see him. Then she gave up, turned and started walking, moving to keep warm. She climbed up the steep slanting road. Maybe if she got high enough she'd get a better view of what Alex was looking at. Her footsteps traced the tire tracks where the car had swerved down the road, even as the lightly blowing snow slowly wiped them away.

She'd lost track of how many times she'd asked God to make Alex a more responsible and serious man. Now she didn't know what to pray. Maybe he was no longer the irresponsible young man she'd once loved. But the mutually supportive relationship that her youthful heart had longed for seemed as far away as ever.

The road grew steeper under her feet. Tire tracks wove in wild curves across the road. She stared down at the muffled patterns of treads on white snow and it took her a moment to understand what she was seeing.

There was a second set of tire tracks ahead on the hill.

She ran toward them. There were two sets of tracks. Two vehicles had started coming down a hill, swerving and jockeying for space. One vehicle had hit the other, sending it flying through the trees, before continuing on down the hill, losing control and crashing. Alex had found the first vehicle. But where was the second one that it had hit? Her eyes scanned the forest. It looked like the driver of the second car had barely managed to steer onto some kind of narrow utility road. She followed it a few steps. Then she saw a faint red light, flickering off and on ahead.

"Alex!" she shouted. "There's a second car!"

She ran toward the blinking light. Her boots pushed through the snow. She could see it now. Zoe's car ahead of her, dented but still intact. She drew closer. The front end was crumpled. The windshield was a shattered mess of cracks. The hazard lights flickered off and on, casting the snow and trees around it in odd red shadows and waves of light.

"Alex!" She cupped around her mouth. "Alex! I've found Zoe's car!"

There was no answer but the wind. She paused, halfway between Zoe's crashed car and the snow-covered road behind her. She could still see the snowmobile between the trees if she craned her neck. If she ran over to the car and checked it out without letting Alex take the lead he'd be frustrated. But what if someone was still in it? What if they needed her help? There were two crashed cars and two of them.

Lord, what do I do?

She walked toward the car cautiously. Even with the hazard lights flashing she could see the splatter of blood on the ground, changing color with the world around it as at the lights blinked off and on. Dark brown against the oddly illuminated red snow. Then bright scarlet on white. She couldn't see anyone in the car. Not from here.

"Hello?" she called. "Is anyone there? Can you hear me?"

She glanced back. Still no Alex. Yes, she had some medical training and was a trauma expert. Due to her role with Victim Services, she'd seen all kinds of tragic accidents and crime scenes. Wisdom told her it was always best to have backup and to never approach the scene of an accident or crime alone. But her only backup had climbed down a hill, by himself, toward a totally different crash.

Help me, Lord. I'm conflicted and I'm doubting myself and I don't even know why.

She stepped closer. The car seemed to be empty. Did that mean Zoe and Mandy had been kidnapped? Did that mean they'd made it out alive?

Then she heard footsteps on the ground and the sound of a handgun's safety clicking off.

"Don't move." A thin, bearded figure lurched into the clearing and leaned heavily against a tree. "Don't even make a sound. Or I'll be forced to shoot you."

FIVE

Wide, bloodshot eyes stared out at her over the folds of a thick scarf. He was wearing a black toque, too, low over his forehead, so the hat and scarf obscured almost all of a bearded face. But he was young. The eyes told her that much. Midtwenties, Theresa guessed. *Who are you?* Someone working for Castor? Someone involved in the ransacking of the cottages and searching for the trunk? Someone from the picture they'd looked at in the cottage? Whoever he was, he wasn't wearing gloves. His legs were shaking, and the bare hand that clutched the gun shook, too. His other hand clenched his side.

"Look, I don't want any trouble!" she said loudly. She wondered just how loud she would need to be for Alex to hear her. "I can see you've got a gun and I don't want to get hurt. I'm just looking for my friends. There were two women in this car. Do you know where they are? Are they okay?"

"I said, be quiet! Okay?" he snapped. "I need to think. You keep it down or I'm going to shoot you. I mean it! I really am going to shoot!"

Would he, though? She wasn't sure. He didn't strike her as a killer. But he struck her as desperate, in pain and in fear. Sometimes that was enough.

"Okay, I hear you." She lowered her voice. Her hands rose slightly in front of her, but more in a posture of defense than surrender. "We can talk quietly. Just set the gun down. I don't want to hurt you, and I'm hoping you don't want to hurt me, either."

"Are you alone? Who are you here with?" His eyes scanned the trees. Muffled questions tumbled from his mouth so quickly his words ran into each other in a garbled mess. "Have you seen Castor? Where is he?"

Even through the scarf she could tell he was sweating and his skin was clammy. He was in pain and on some kind of heavy pain-killers, too, probably far higher than a legal dose. Would he even be able make the shot, from a distance like that, with his limbs shaking that badly? Maybe. It was hard to tell. If

Alex didn't materialize soon, she might have to handle this on her own.

She was familiar with guns. Comfortable with them, too. But handgun licenses were so hard to come by in Canada that his weapon was almost certainly illegal. Most of the families on the lake hunted with shotguns and rifles. Paul Wright had killed his first deer when he was just fourteen. Not to mention, she'd done more than her fair share of lessons at the local gun club in the past few weeks, after a maniac had threatened her and her friend Samantha at Christmas.

But none of that had managed to prepare her for snatching one from a criminal's hand.

Help me, Lord. What do I do? I'm a psychotherapist, not a bodyguard.

"I asked you where Castor is!" he snapped. He pulled his hand away from his side long enough to adjust his grip on the gun and she could see a thick smear of blood on his hands. His side was bleeding. Had he been shot? Stabbed? "What did Castor tell you?"

Her eyes rose from the weapon to the young man holding it. Despite the fear in her chest, something like pity still wrenched inside her heart. Whoever he was, whatever he'd done, he needed help. If she got him talking, maybe she could get him to drop his weapon or stall him long enough for Alex to find her.

"I'm sorry, I honestly don't know where Castor is," she said. She took a slow step forward. "You're hurt. Is it a gunshot? A knife wound? If you tell me, I can help you take care of it. I have a first aid kit in my bag." He didn't respond. "Look, you need medical attention. I need to find my friends and get them home safely. So how about you put down the gun and let me help you?"

He raised the gun in his shaky hands. "Don't come any closer."

She stopped. His aim might be terrible and he might not be able to hit her on the first shot, but that didn't mean he wasn't willing to die trying. "Look, I don't know what kind of trouble you and your friends are in—"

"Castor's not my friend!" He spat in the snow, then let out a long string of swearwords, letting her know what kind of low-level piece of scum he thought Castor and those like him were. It wasn't pretty. "Now, tell me, what does Castor know?"

"I don't work for Castor! He's not my friend, either!" She could feel her voice rising in her chest, but she bit it back and forced it level, as if she was trying to calm a wild animal. "I don't even know what you want to know or what you're trying to ask me. I was at the Rhodeses' family cottage. Number Eight on the lake. Castor broke in with two cronies and trashed the place. He said their names were Howler and Brick... Brick was shot."

His hand tightened on the gun. "By who? Who shot him?"

"I don't know for sure. Castor, I think. I'm sorry, but Brick didn't make it."

His face grew paler. "And Castor didn't mention me?"

"I'm sorry. I don't know if he mentioned you because I don't know who you are. Have we met before? My name is Theresa Vaughan. My family used to have a cottage on the lake."

He shrugged. His eyes scanned the forest around her. Okay, so that wasn't exactly a "no" to the question of whether or not they'd met before. But if they had, it had been a long time ago, when he was much younger. He might not even remember her. His hand pressed deeper into his side. She stretched one hand out, just a little, as if showing him an open door in the air between them and welcoming him to walk through it.

"You can call me Theresa," she said softly. "I help people who are in trouble. And you are?"

He grimaced and didn't meet her eye. "Castor calls me Gnat. Like the bug."

Gnat? At least "Brick" had made sense because it had been the young man's last name. But she couldn't think of anybody connected to Cedar Lake that had a name that sounded like *gnat* or was anything close to any kind of insect. His eyes twitched like he was struggling to think. She cast a quick glance at the sky. The flakes falling from above were growing thicker.

"Look, I don't know how badly you're hurt or what happened here," she said. "But I do know that you're bleeding, a storm is coming and it's going to take us a very long time to get to the hospital. I don't have a car. Do you?"

"I hitchhiked and walked." He shook his head. "Castor ran my car off the road and I crashed. I was trying to make this one go."

Okay, she guessed that would be the one that Alex had climbed down to see. Not that his hitchhiking comment made any sense for now. Maybe the combination of pain and pain medication was muddying his brain.

"I'm going to walk over to my friend's car and see if I can make it go. Okay?"

He didn't answer. Slowly she stepped closer, praying with every step. The driver's door was open. Empty wires hung where the ignition had been. The front passenger's seat was slashed diagonally from one corner to the other. Carefully she opened the passenger's door and looked closer. The cut in the seat was so deep the corner of the seat had been hastily hacked off. A few quick lines had been scratched on the dashboard forming the letters *A* and *Y*. An odd beat of hope clattered in her chest.

When she was a teenager, *A* and *Y* were a secret signal she, Alex, Zoe and Josh had used on their scavenger hunts. It was their short form for the question "Are we a team?" and the response, "Yes, we're the best team ever!"

They'd used those two lines as secret signals to each other, a long, long time ago. Could Zoe be trying to remind her of that now?

"Who cut up the car like this?" She straightened up. "Was it you? Was it Castor?"

"I don't want to talk about Castor!" A burst of fresh swearing from Gnat filled the air and her mind, drowning out her ability to think. The pain in his side must be growing worse. "I did everything Castor asked me to do. Everything! But he kept pushing for more and more, and using me and making me do things I didn't want to do."

An odd sadness for the men caught in whatever vicious game they were playing filled her chest. If Brick had been nothing more to Castor than a hired hand, it would definitely explain how ready they had been to turn on each other.

"Did he send you up here to look for a trunk?" she asked.

"What do you know about the trunk?" Gnat's voice suddenly rose to a howl. He ran across the snow toward her, before she could react, raised the gun and pointed it right between her eyes. "Who told you about the trunk? Who?"

"Castor." Her heart beat hard in her chest. What had she done? "He ransacked the Rhodeses' family cottage looking for it."

The profanity that left Gnat's mouth was so vile it was almost painful. "I'm going to kill him."

"Look," Theresa said, "if you want to stop him, please just tell me who he is and what he's done. We'll go to the police. We'll make sure he faces justice."

"Don't you get it? Castor is above the law. Police can't stop him!"

Oh, if she had a nickel for every paranoid criminal who didn't trust the police to help them.

"Nothing can stop Castor." Gnat's voice rose. "Nothing but that trunk. And I'm not going to risk me and mine by telling you who he is. You'll run to the police. They'll do nothing. He'll figure out I blabbed his identity and get his revenge. Castor has a way of finding things out. But he doesn't know where the trunk is. And I'm thinking maybe you do."

"Me?" Why would he ever think that? "No! I have no idea where the trunk is!"

His lip curled. "Well, someone thinks you can help find it."

What? "Who? Castor?"

"I'm done talking. Get in the car." He gestured toward the vehicle with the barrel of his weapon. "We're going to go find Castor and kill him. That's the only way this will ever end and we'll ever be free. Then, after he's dead, you are going to help find the trunk. Then, after that, depending on how that goes, I might let you go free. But either way, I'm taking you with me."

Alex stood with his feet braced on the side of the snow-covered hillside, the frozen lake spread out below him. The remains of the wrecked sports car hung suspended between a tree and rock above him. Spent bullets and shattered glass littered the snowy ground. His legs ached. He'd been carefully tiptoeing around this wreck for far too long. Theresa was sure to be bored and frustrated waiting for him. But the moment he'd seen the blood staining the snow around the crashed car he knew this was something he needed to handle alone.

There was a body in the driver's seat of the car. The young man was suspended upside down from the force of the seat belt restraint. He was very thin, in his early twenties, and most definitely dead from the gunshot wound to his chest. Balancing carefully on the precarious rocks, Alex had carefully taken a photograph of the man's face and the wreckage surrounding him. Then he gingerly reached into the dead man's pocket and pulled out his wallet.

Blake Howler. Twenty-one. From Stoney Creek, Ontario.

Howler. The same name as one of Castor's men. Alex prayed the death had been quick and merciful.

From what he could piece together, the vehicle had spun off the road, rolled down the hill and then been shot to pieces by some kind of semiautomatic handgun, killing the driver in the process. He could only guess why. Was Castor getting rid of another potential rival for the notorious treasure trunk? Had he been killed by somebody else? The side of the hill was such a mess of snow and scrub he couldn't even begin to make a good guess about how many people had been in the car when it had crashed or where exactly they'd gone.

Alex stepped carefully from a rock to a tree stump and listened to the howl of the rising wind. "Hang on, just one more second, Theresa. I'm almost done."

She didn't answer. He frowned. It'd been way too long since he'd heard her voice. As thankful as he was that she hadn't followed him down the hill, the thought of her waiting alone by the snowmobile wasn't exactly a comforting one, either.

That moment when she'd almost tackled him with a hug from behind at the Pattersons' cottage stirred up more, even less pleasant memories the more the thought about it. He winced. He'd abandoned her and gone off on his own to have adventures with other kids on the lake too many times when they were younger. He hadn't excluded her out of malice. She just hadn't been as fast a runner or as strong a swimmer, and had a tendency to point out when the things he was doing were reckless. Emmett and Kyle Rhodes, especially, were the kind of guys who'd hit him up on the spur of the moment for some wild and crazy adventure, and hadn't been that thrilled when Alex had gotten a girlfriend. So he'd bail on her, sometimes on a moment's notice. Sometimes she'd caught up to him, leaped on his back and hugged him long enough to make him stop and say goodbye. Sometimes she'd just let him go.

He just prayed she understood that telling her to stay back and stay out of his way this time was entirely professional and not the slightest bit personal. As was his desire to drop her off as soon as possible and find Zoe and Mandy solo.

Despite the awfully fast, off-kilter heartbeat she still seemed to cause deep in his chest cavity.

He looked up. "Theresa? I'm on my way up."

Still no answer. The snow had started falling heavily again, coming down in bursts of scattered flakes. He leaped up two rocks, then grabbed hold of a sapling and started climbing, heading for a large tree growing almost diagonally out of the slope.

Snow slid under his feet. Wind beat against him. He took another step up and slid back three. He pulled his scarf over his face all the way up to his nose and wished he hadn't left his snowmobile helmet behind. His blue-gray eyes rose to the ridge above. Where was she? For the first time a shiver of fear brushed his spine. She wouldn't have wandered off, would she? Theresa had always been sensible and levelheaded. He'd never met anyone more grounded. Then why hadn't he trusted her enough to let her climb down? True, the slope was dangerous. But surely she'd have been careful.

"Hey, you didn't happen to pack a rope in that kit of yours, did you?" he called up. "Not to be overly dramatic, but the ground is pretty steep. I wouldn't mind something to hold on to if you can find a tree to tie some rope around." Plus the wind wasn't helping any. "Hey, Theresa? You there?"

A scream for help rose on the air, stiffening his spine and filling his heart with dread.

Theresa was in danger. His hands scrambled in the snow.

"Theresa!" He shouted, his voice hoarse in the cold air. "Hold on! I'm coming!"

Deep and heavy snow dragged his footsteps backward. His legs ached. His heart pounded like a fist inside his rib cage. He tried to scramble around the car, but couldn't catch a grip.

"Alex! Help!"

He grabbed the twisted bumper and hoisted himself up onto the car. The car groaned beneath him. A gunshot split the air. *God, please help me reach her in time!*

SIX

The unstable car shook beneath his feet. Carefully he made his way across the undercarriage of the overturned car, then braced his legs and reached up. The tree was just a few inches out of his grasp. The car groaned beneath his weight, threatening at any moment to hurtle down the hill, before plunging down into the frozen lake below, taking him with it. He bent his legs, knowing he'd only get one try. Then he leaped.

The car fell away from under him. His hands grasped the tree trunk above him and held on tightly. He could hear the crash of metal and glass as the car slid down the hill, then the crack of ice as it smashed its way through. His arms tightened around the tree trunk. His legs swung in the empty air. Prayers for help and of thanksgiving mingled on his lips. Then, slowly and carefully, he hauled his body up around the tree, onto more even ground, and propelled his legs up the hill.

He reached the empty road. Theresa was nowhere to be seen. The whistle of wind filled his ears and the sound of tree branches beat above him like a chorus of wooden drumsticks.

He cupped his hands and shouted her name into the wind.

For a long, agonizing moment he heard no response. Then the sound of her screaming his name filled his ears, and he saw her pelting down the icy road toward him.

He ran for her.

A second gunshot blast echoed in the trees. Then a bearded figure appeared behind her, his face obscured by a hat and scarf. His fist caught Theresa on the side of the head. She pitched forward and landed hard on her hands and knees.

"Stay back!" The man yanked her head up as she knelt on the icy road in front of him. "Stay back or I'll kill her. I'm not joking. I'll do it!"

Alex's feet skidded to a halt, not twenty paces away from where Theresa now knelt on the frozen earth. A deep breath filled her lungs and he watched her wince with the effort of gasping in a deep, cold breath.

"There are letters in Zoe's car!" she shouted. Her voice rose as she pushed it through her lips. "*A* and *Y. A* and *Y!*"

The gunman yanked her head back. Her words froze on her lips. Alex's heart froze in his throat. He didn't know what she was talking about.

"Are we a team?" She looked up at him. Her hood fell back. "Remember? Are we a team?"

She wasn't making any sense. Were they a team? If he said they were, there was the possibility that she would do something reckless to put her life in further danger.

He couldn't let that happen. He took a deep breath and lifted his gaze to the man now holding a gun to the back of Theresa's head.

"Who are you?" Alex called down the frozen road. "What do you want?"

"I'm Gnat." The young man's teeth were chattering. "I need the trunk."

"We don't have it," Alex shouted back. He shrugged broadly, hoping the gesture would help get the message through to him. "I know a lot of people want it. But I don't know where it is."

Gnat paused.

"He's telling the truth," Theresa said. "We don't know what it looks like or even what's inside."

The young man hesitated. He glanced from Theresa to Alex. "I've got to go find it!"

"Okay, we won't stop you. Just lower your weapon and go." Alex took a step forward. His hands rose. "Hey, take my snowmobile if you want."

The gun shook in the young man's hands. Theresa's eyes closed and Alex could see her lips move in silent prayer. Fear was building in Alex's chest, pressing painfully inside him with every heartbeat.

"Trust me! I don't want the trunk. I just care about Theresa. I'm willing to settle this peacefully. But this is your last warning." An edge moved through his voice, like the glimmer of a knife's blade. "Drop the gun, raise your hands and let Theresa go!"

"Not until I settle things with Castor!" Gnat shouted. "She might be my only hope of finding it." The gun clicked. A bullet blasted, tearing up the snow inches away from Theresa's body. Snow and debris filled Alex's eyes. "Look, I'm not playing around!"

Neither was he. Alex sprinted across the

snow toward the gunman. His eyes locked on Theresa's form, praying with each step that she was all right, and that she hadn't been shot. The snow cleared. Theresa's eyes met his, filled with determination and fire. Gnat cocked the gun. But before he could fire, Theresa reached up both hands over her shoulder and grabbed Gnat's gun. *What was she doing?* "Theresa! Baby! Don't!"

Gnat's curses filled the air. Theresa yanked the gun hard over her shoulder, pulling Gnat forward with it, taking him off balance. Then she turned toward him. Rising up on one knee, she tried to twist the gun from his grasp. Gnat fell on top of her. They struggled for the gun.

Alex skidded to a stop. He couldn't leap into the fight. Not without knowing where the gun was. There was too big a possibility that he could accidentally set it off, killing her. For an agonizing second, he watched them fight, battling the urge to leap in and tear them apart as it swelled inside him like a tidal wave. Then he saw the gun flash in Gnat's hand. A bullet ricocheted into the trees. Gnat scrambled to his feet and dashed up the hill into the woods.

Theresa lay crumpled in the snow, her body curled up in a ball.

Oh, please. No. Alex landed by her side.

His hand reached for her, his trembling fingers brushed against her shoulder. *Please, she has to be okay. I can't lose her again.*

Pain filled Theresa's skull. Her ears rang and spots filled her eyes as she lay there for a moment, pressed against the cold, frozen rocks of the unpaved cottage road. She was dizzy. She could still smell the blood from Gnat's jacket and the smoke from his gun. When he'd first tried to force her into the car, she'd managed to level a good elbow shot to his injured side and run. But she'd lost her footing, which slowed her down just long enough to let him catch up to her again. And when she'd fought him for the gun, he'd managed to strike her so hard she nearly lost consciousness.

"Theresa! Baby! Talk to me. Please."

She could hear Alex's voice, calling her *baby*, pleading with her to answer. But it was like she was drifting on the edge of consciousness, caught between awake and asleep. Maybe she was imagining it. He hadn't called her baby in so very long. Her eyes closed.

Lord, please don't let me pass out.

There was so much Alex still didn't know. He didn't know about Zoe's car just a few steps away up the hill and around the corner.

He didn't know that Gnat was like a cornered rat in a cage who didn't know how to fight his way out. He didn't seem to understand what she'd been trying to say about seeing the letters scratched in Zoe's car and how it had reminded her of their old scavenger hunts.

He didn't know just how very much she'd missed him or that she had never stopped caring for him.

Slowly she pushed herself up onto her hands and knees, fighting the nausea threatening to pull her down. She ran her cold, wet hands over her face. Her eyes opened.

Alex was crouched on the road beside her. His face hovered inches away from hers.

His hand touched her shoulder. "Are you okay? Were you shot?"

"I'm okay." She forced a smile. "Just dizzy. But I'll be fine. Go after him. Zoe's car's in the woods up ahead on a utility road—"

His touch stiffened as tension filled his fingers. "What about Zoe and Mandy?"

"She wasn't in the car," Theresa said. "Neither was Mandy. The car's empty. But I think she slashed the seat with her knife and scratched letters in the dashboard."

Alex stood. For a moment his legs tensed, as if he was about to spring and run after

Gnat. She heard him whisper a prayer under his breath. Then he stopped and knelt down on one knee beside her in the snow. Gently he took her hands. "You're bleeding."

Was she? She looked down. The palms of her gloves were singed from grabbing the still-smoking gun and there was blood streaking the sleeves of her coat.

"That's not my blood. It's Gnat's. His side was bleeding. I think Castor shot him or stabbed him. He wouldn't tell me for sure." She bent down, grabbed a handful of snow and vigorously wiped it off. Apparently she'd misjudged both how injured he was and how strong. "He's too scared of Castor to tell me who he is. He thinks even the police can't stop Castor."

"It's not surprising that a criminal doesn't trust the police," Alex said.

True enough.

"I don't know why he thought I could help him find the trunk," she added. "He said someone told him I knew something about it. But he wouldn't tell me who. I'm guessing it was Castor."

Brick had thought she could help find it, too.

Once again she expected Alex to leap up

and run. Instead, his hand brushed along the side of her face. "Are you sure you're okay, though? How's your head?"

"I'm a bit dizzy. I told you. But I'm fine," she said. Not to mention she was frustrated she'd even let Gnat get a punch in. "Don't worry about me. Go after him. Find out what he knows. He's frightened and desperate. Not to mention hopped-up on painkillers. But he fired at me twice and missed each time. Which is why I knew I could fight for the gun, before he risked actually shooting one of us. I think he'd only kill if he was cornered and had no choice."

Alex still didn't move. His fingers lingered on her face. What was he doing? Sure, most people she knew would choose to stay with someone they knew instead of chasing a criminal through the trees. She, for one, would pick that every time. But not Alex. The Alex she'd fallen in love with couldn't stay still for a moment and never missed an opportunity to run after anything dangerous and exciting.

Instead, here he was, still kneeling beside her, turning her hands over in his, as if he was making doubly sure that she really was as okay as she said she was. His fingertips ran over her arms so tenderly that even through layers of a sweatshirt and winter jacket she shivered as if he'd touched her bare skin.

"I'd thought he'd shot you." Alex leaned his forehead against hers. Somehow feeling him there felt just as intimate as if he'd kissed her.

She swallowed hard. "Well, he didn't."

An engine roared. Gnat had gotten the car to start. They leaped to their feet, as Zoe's blue car shot out of the woods and careened down the hill toward them. Gnat had obviously hit the accelerator hard and had no idea how to control the vehicle on the ice, and now it was sliding sideways down the road.

The car spun as Gnat lost control of the wheel.

It was going to hit them.

Alex threw his arms around Theresa, clutching her to his chest. They rolled sideways. His body wrapped around hers like a protective shell. She heard the rumble of the engine and Alex's breath coming hard and fast in her ear.

Then they were over the edge of the cliff, tumbling down into the trees toward the frozen lake below.

SEVEN

They were rolling. Their bodies were plummeting down the hill toward the lake, and all Alex could do was hold onto Theresa, shelter her with his body and pray. He closed his eyes. Rocks and branches beat against him. Then they hit a pocket of deep snow and their bodies sank into it. He felt thick coniferous branches smack against him. They stopped rolling.

"Thank You, Lord."

He heard a prayer slip through Theresa's lips and felt her hot breath on his cold skin. He opened his eyes. They were lying side by side, half buried in the snow. A huge pine tree pressed against his back. Theresa's nose was just inches from his. Her hands clutched his coat. His arms were wrapped around her body. The rumbling sound of Zoe's car engine disappeared down the road above them. A prayer of gratitude filled his heart. He pulled back slightly and felt the snow shifting around them. "Are you okay? How's your head?"

"I'm fine. Thanks." Theresa leaned away, out of his arms, and craned her head to look down the hill past them. "Well, that could've been worse."

"Don't move." His arms tightened around her. He could feel the tension deepening his voice, making him sound a lot more like a bodyguard than an ex-boyfriend holding the woman he once thought he'd marry in his arms. "We've got to be careful. The last thing we want to do is shift too much ground and end up falling farther down the hill."

"All right." She stopped moving.

Was it his imagination, or was she arching her back away from him, as if the last place she wanted to be right now was in his arms?

"Are you sure you're okay?" he asked. "You're not hurt?"

"I'm not hurt. Just let me know when I can climb out of here." Her jaw was clenched so tightly that tension practically radiated through her skin. Was she upset with him for some reason? Frustrated? For a second he just lay there, feeling her heart beating against his chest and the snow swirling down around them, while he argued down the impulse to ask her if she was upset with him. But it didn't matter. They were stuck on a snowy hillside, having just been run off the road by a criminal, and as long as he got her out of here safely and alive it didn't much matter whether or not she liked him.

No matter how much Theresa might still push one or two of his buttons.

She shifted. Her arms brushed against his chest. A shiver ran through him.

All right, she still pushed a whole lot of his buttons—starting with the one telling him he needed to protect her.

"Okay, so, here's what's going to happen," he said. "You're going to get to your feet, very slowly and carefully, and then see if you can find anything above you to grab on to. I'll steady your legs. Got it?"

"Got it." Theresa crawled up onto her hands and knees slowly. "I've got nowhere to put my feet."

"Put your feet on my hands. Use my palms like a step stool." He shifted onto his back. "I can support you."

She planted her boot firmly into his palm. His right hand gripped her calf, feeling the unexpected strength of her muscles through her ski pants. Then he lifted her up as high as he could. The weight of her body pushed his down hard against the pine tree. He could hear the branches creak. She gasped a deep breath.

"Okay, I've found a handhold. Let me go." She pulled her leg up out of his grasp.

He stayed there, watching the soles of her boots grow smaller as she climbed up the hill above him. "You good?"

"I'm great." Her voice filtered down. "When you stand up, you'll see a bush above you to the right and a solid rock just above that to your left. It's not super great for footholds. But the road's only about twenty feet up and it's not that bad a climb. I'm almost there." She disappeared from view. Snow and sky filled his view. Then her head appeared above him over the ledge. "I'm good! All safe. Come on up."

He said a prayer that was half thanksgiving and half a plea for help, for guidance. Then he started climbing after her. *Wow.* Theresa had been optimistic in describing the climb as not that bad. The climb was steeper than the one he'd tackled earlier on a different part of the slope, and with fewer hand-and footholds. Definitely not impossible, by any means, especially not to an experienced athlete with his kind of upper body strength. But not the kind of challenge he'd have ever expected Theresa to tackle so cheerfully.

His grip tightened on a rock hidden under the surface of the snow.

"Need a hand?" Theresa was still looking down at him over the edge, with a gentle, kindhearted smile that told him she was trying her best not to let whatever negative feelings were bubbling inside her show on the outside. She'd always been like that. Quick to hide whatever was upsetting her. Even quicker to forgive. He knew that smile too well and had probably ignored it more times than he was comfortable admitting.

"Nah, I've got it." Alex hauled himself over the ledge and back up to the road. "Where's the snowmobile?"

"In the trees on the other side of the road." She pointed. "Gnat definitely clipped it. But thankfully he sent it flying toward the rocks instead of over the cliff."

He strode in the direction she'd indicated. The snowmobile was dented in the front. But thankfully nothing was leaking and the skis weren't bent. He pulled it back onto the road and tried the engine. It started.

"Looks like we're good to go," he said.

She frowned. He knew she probably still wanted to talk about what she thought she'd seen in Zoe's car, and he definitely still needed to tell her about the body he'd discovered in the totaled sports car that was now sinking into the icy waters of the lake. But he was tired of talking. He was tired of things going wrong. He was tired of feeling stuck. He was tired of being out in the cold and the snow, watching the flakes grow thicker. He had to get her to the safe house.

"We need to think carefully and plan where we're going from here," Theresa said. "I just wish you'd gotten to the car before Gnat."

Okay, now he definitely heard an edge of frustration in her voice. One that even verged on desperation. His jaw clenched.

Help me, God. I don't know what to do. If I ignore whatever she's going through and push her to get back on the snowmobile, she probably won't argue with me. I don't want to be that kind of man anymore. But I also don't want to stand around talking when we should be taking action, especially if standing around puts her in even more danger.

"We need to get out of here, and quickly." He turned the snowmobile off again. "But I can tell something's bothering you. So, let's just take five seconds and talk it out quick. But just five. No more. I'm sorry if I was too rough and sudden when I grabbed you like that and we rolled off the cliff. I was trying to save your life. I didn't exactly have a choice."

"I get that." She shook her head. "But you could've just left me and chased after Gnat. You might've even stopped him from taking Zoe's car."

"You were hurt. You were down on the ground! That was all that mattered. Not some car. You, baby, I care about you!"

The words flew from his lips and seemed to echo around them, swirling in the snow and bouncing off the trees.

Baby, I care about you.

I. Care. About. You.

Her green eyes opened wide. But the surprise on her face was nothing compared to the shock he felt. What was he saying? What's more, what was he thinking? He hadn't called her baby in years. Not since the day she'd shattered his heart. But that was three times the word had slipped out of his mouth without even thinking.

"Sorry, I shouldn't have called you that," he said. "Of course you matter. You're my sister's friend, you're our client's psychotherapist and you're an important asset for Ash Private Security. Obviously, you were an important part of my past, too. That goes without saying."

Her lips parted slightly. But no words came out. Instead, she bit her lip, reminding him of every kiss he'd ever given her.

"Yes, you're right it was unfortunate that Gnat stole Zoe's car." He kept talking, like maybe if he got enough words out in a row somehow he'd hit upon the right ones. "But at the end of the day, a car is just a car. You're still you."

Static and buzzing filled the air. A disjointed voice faded in and out over the air. He blinked, then fumbled for the CB radio on his belt. He hadn't even realized it was still on. But he was insanely thankful it was still working.

"Hello?" He raised it to his lips. "Is anybody there?"

"Break, break. Is anyone there?" A girl's voice filtered through the distorted channel.

"It's the kid," Alex said. Theresa reached for the CB radio. But Alex sheltered the radio with his hand from the elements. "Hi. You're Bug, right? Beetle? Something like that? I need you to go get your parents for me. Right now. It's very important. I don't know how long I'm going to have a signal and we need the police."

"You're a rude man," the girl said. "I don't want to talk to you."

"Just let me talk to her." Again, Theresa reached for the CB.

But Alex didn't even seem to notice.

"Look, kid, I'm really not trying to be rude." He sighed. "But we're dealing with some major, grown-up stuff here. Please, just go get your parents, right now. They've got to call the police about what's going on at Cedar Lake."

"I'm not supposed to tell stories about that!" The girl's voice grew sharp. "Nobody believes any of it anyway. They say it's all just a prank."

"What did you just say?" Alex asked. "What did you mean by a prank? Nobody believes what?"

"Don't talk to me again. Over and out." The line went to static.

Alex groaned. They'd found precisely one CB channel with a person on the other end they could potentially ask for help, and it was being manned by a child who refused to talk to them. "Tell me that you're as worried as I am that she refused to talk to us about what's happening up here because people think it's a 'prank.'"

"I am," Theresa admitted, "Especially considering Gnat's convinced that Castor's somehow above the law. Although, judging by her tone of voice, I'm relieved to say I don't think that child's in any physical danger. I think she's at a house far away from the lake, as she said earlier, and just going through random radio channels looking for someone. I'm also glad that whoever her parents are, they seem to have taught her some great self-protection skills. That bodes well for her, too."

"I can't believe you're praising a child for cutting me off, refusing to talk to me." He clipped the CB radio back to his belt. "Although I totally see your point that it's a good thing a child knows better than to talk to a stranger about something she's upset about—especially not a rude man."

Despite herself, she felt a smile brush her lips. "I agree that if we happen to reach her again, we need to try to talk her into putting a responsible adult on the line."

"We need to make sure somebody calls the police. We have a criminal on the loose up here who's apparently willing to kill indiscriminately, not to mention two dead bodies."

The smile fell from her lips "Two?"

"There was a body in the driver's seat of the car that crashed down the hill." He pulled his cell phone out of his zippered jacket pocket. The phone screen was a mass of cracks. But thankfully it still turned on. He held up a picture. "His name was Blake Howler. He was twenty-one and from Stoney Creek. Is this the same Howler who was with Castor and Brick?"

"I think so." Her face paled. He'd been the one who'd called her a finicky princess. But she'd never seen him before. Maybe he'd heard someone else call her that? Castor had said something similar about her, too. She sighed. Something about this whole thing still felt personal. But she couldn't put a finger on why or how. "So, Castor killed both the men who helped him break into the cottage? I don't even know what that means. Or why someone would do that."

"Maybe he found the trunk he was after and was trying to eliminate his rivals to avoid paying them their share."

She shuddered. "Or maybe we were wrong

this whole time and Castor didn't kill them. Maybe whoever else is after the trunk did."

Two warring gangs, each searching for the same cache—of drugs, or weapons, or whatever else people were willing to kill each other for—was the kind of thing she'd expect to hear about happening in a crime-heavy part of a big city. Not at the idyllic Northern Ontario lake where she'd spent her childhood summers.

"Change of plans," he said. "You might've noticed that when we reached the fork in the road earlier, I didn't turn toward my cottage and instead kept going toward the highway. That's because Zoe and I set up an emergency meeting place. Mandy Rhodes's older brother Emmett recently bought a broken-down house on an offshoot of the lake. It's completely dilapidated and in need of repair, so it wasn't intended as any kind of shelter. But if anything went disastrously wrong, Zoe was supposed to take Mandy there, as a last-case scenario, and hide out until Daniel or myself could retrieve her. I'm hoping that, when we get there, we'll find Zoe and Mandy waiting for us. But if we don't, I'm going to suggest that we find a safe corner there for you to hide in while I head down the highway and see if I can get a phone signal or flag down some help."

"But I told you I saw letters scratched on the dashboard of the car," she said. "The letter *A* and the letter *Y*, along with a diagonal slash in the seat. I'm pretty sure it's a message from Zoe."

"Okay, well, if it's a message from her, we can figure out what it means at the safe house."

"No." She shook her head. "We need to follow them now. Remember, back when we were teenagers, the year we won the scavenger hunt? We didn't want to risk any of the other teams hearing us talking on the radio. So we came up with the idea of making some signal out of twigs, or rocks or scuff marks on the ground, to let each other know where we'd gone. I'd suggested it be the letters *A* and *Y* because you kept trying to gear us up for victory going, 'Are we a team? Are we a team?'"

"And you'd say, 'Yeah, we're the best team ever.'" His voice trailed off. "If you're right, and it is a sign from Zoe, then what way do you think she wanted us to go?"

She stretched her hand out and pointed out across the lake, in the same direction that the knife slash in the seat had run, toward the tip of the giant outcropping of rock on her parents' old property. It was the place where Alex had proposed. It was the place they were supposed to have gotten married. If Zoe had been trying to get her attention, there was no better place on Cedar Lake to point her toward. Surely Alex would get that, too. Wouldn't he?

But, instead, he chuckled.

She pressed her lips together. "You're laughing at me."

"No, sorry, I was laughing at the irony of the situation." He ran his hand over his head. "Because that's the opposite direction of where I'm trying to take you. There's nothing even in that direction except a useless hunk of rock."

It wasn't a hunk. It was a beautiful, long, flat slab of Canadian Shield granite spreading out into the lake like a natural dock. Her cottage had been on the crest of the hill. The rock had been beneath them at the very edge of their beach, down steep winding stairs her father had built.

"That rock was on my parents' property." Her arms tightened across her chest. "It's the rock we were supposed to get married on."

"A million years ago!" he exclaimed. "There's no reason why Zoe would ever want to remind us of something so disastrous and painful. We're not kids anymore. There could be any number of reasons why there were scratches on the dashboard of the car, and they happen to look like letters.

"Okay, so maybe I didn't used to be the most reliable guy. But that's not who I am anymore. I take my work very seriously. Ash Private Security has plans in place for dealing with emergencies. Ones that don't involve random knife scratches and chasing obscure clues through the woods in a storm. Snow is still falling, with a lot more coming. I have no idea why we haven't seen any sign of police yet or what that girl on the radio could've possibly meant by a prank. But thankfully the snowmobile seems to be running so we have a possibility of getting out of here while the road is still passable. There's no way to get to that rock without either walking through the woods or taking the snowmobile out on the lake, neither of which is wise. I'm taking you to the safe house."

"And if Zoe and Mandy aren't there?" Her chin rose.

"Then I'm going to make sure it's safe, leave you there and go find help," he said.

"But Zoe obviously tried to come back this

way not that long ago," she said. "The hazard lights were still flashing. Clearly she's not at the rendezvous point."

"Or somebody else stole her car while she was in town and she never came back to the lake," Alex said. "Or she tried to come back for you, crashed the car, and then did what any sensible bodyguard would do after being run off the road and shot at by killers, and took her client to the place where we'd agreed to meet."

"But if we get to the safe house and they're not there, your plan is to just leave me there," she said. "You don't think I can help. But Gnat and Brick tried to force me to help them find the trunk. They thought I knew where it was or had some connection to it."

"But you don't," he said. "You'll be safer hiding in an abandoned-looking, derelict house that they're very, very unlikely to decide to search, instead of us zooming off through the woods toward some open slab of rock, in front of the very big, beautiful and obviously expensive cottage you used to live in." He shook his head. "I don't get where this is coming from. You're the most sensible person I've ever met. You're the last person who'd ever tell me to do something like this."

"Then shouldn't that tell you something?" Theresa stepped toward him. Her gloved hands brushed his forearms. His arms parted as if, despite his frustration, something inside him still wanted to wrap his arms tight around her and lift her into his chest. "You used to say, 'Baby, you're the brains and I'm the brawn. You make all the plans. I'll do all the things.' How many times did you make that joke?"

He didn't answer for a long moment. They stood there, so close she could see their breaths mingling in the winter air. Then his spine straightened. He took a step back.

"I remember," he said. "I remember everything. But I'm not that guy anymore. I'm not your boyfriend or your fiancé or your adventurous friend or your scavenger hunt teammate. I'm Zoe's colleague, Mandy's bodyguard and the man who's going to do what needs to be done to keep you alive, whether you like it or not. Now, you can choose to get on the snowmobile with me, or you can choose to go your own way on foot, because I can't actually force you onto a snowmobile. But I'm not going to let some distant memory of the relationship we used to have a very long time ago sabotage what I came up here to do."

"You're right." She stepped back, too. The past was over. She knew that better than anyone. Alex had moved on with his life. So why was something inside her still trying to grasp what might've been? "I didn't mean to imply I wasn't taking this seriously, or that I didn't respect the difficult position you're in. Or to bring up things we're probably both better off forgetting. Yes, I think Zoe was sending us a message. Yes, I think she wants us to head across the lake to my family's old property. But I'm not going to stand here, on an open road, in the snow, arguing about it. Obviously I'm not going to set off alone, on foot through the snow, either. We'll go with your plan and I hope you're right. Just give me a second to go get my backpack."

"Thank you" was all he said. But even though she'd just agreed with him there was a sadness to his voice that twisted something deep inside her chest. She was cooperating. Alex had won the argument. What more did he want?

They walked back to where Zoe's car had been. Thankfully Theresa's backpack was still there, tossed into the brush near where she'd first fought with Gnat. Alex took a few photographs of the tire tracks, but between the falling snow and the chaos it was hard to figure out how many sets of footprints there'd been. But one thing was clear—there were no tracks heading in the direction she thought Zoe wanted them to go. Maybe she'd been wrong.

They got on the snowmobile and continued north, the sound of the snowmobile rumbling beneath them. The late afternoon sky grew darker. Snow fell heavily. Wind whistled around them seeming to cut straight through her clothes. She kept her hands steady on his waist and fought the urge to pull him close for warmth. He steered off the frozen road and onto an almost-hidden trail that cut through the woods. Thick chunks of ice the size of jagged boulders lined their path. Snow laden trees leaned heavily over the trail.

Then the trees parted and an old farmhouse loomed out of the trees ahead. She felt Alex breathe a sigh of relief. He cut the engine at the edge of the woods.

"Stay here, okay?" He slid off the snowmobile. "I just want to make sure everything's okay."

He crossed a large driveway toward the derelict house. The place was huge and, judging by the road to her left, it seemed to be attached to the main highway by a long private road. Gaping windows of broken glass loomed above them like mouthfuls of broken teeth. Emmett the car salesman owned this place? She stood up and stepped off the snowmobile, letting her aching body stretch and her frozen limbs move to get some heat back into them. She couldn't begin to guess what kind of money it would take to bring a property this large back to life.

She watched as Alex crept along the side of the building. A window was open by the back door. Then his steps froze, his eyes searched the ground and he turned and started back to Theresa.

She stepped toward him. "Is everything okay?" she called.

He shook his head. His finger rose to his mouth hushing her. Her voice froze.

There was a bang to his right. A figure in a dark ski mask burst out the back door.

"Theresa, get out of here!" Alex pelted toward the snowmobile. "It's a—"

The world exploded around him, throwing

him to the ground in a blaze of flames and broken wood, before her mind could even find the word *trap*.

EIGHT

The safe house exploded. Theresa watched in horror as a cascade of flames and flaming debris seemed to swallow Alex whole. *Help him, Lord!* Tears filled her eyes. Panicked prayers filled her voice. Then the smoke parted and she saw him. Alex's hands rose as a tall, masked man held a rifle to his chest. *Castor?* With a move so quick she could barely see how, Alex leaped to the side, twisted the rifle up in the air and snapped it clear out of the masked man's hands. The weapon flew into the flames.

"Theresa!" Alex's voice rose through the smoke. "Get out of here!"

Castor's fist flew at Alex's face. Alex ducked. Then he dived, catching Castor hard with an elbow to the jaw. All she could see was a flurry of fists and blows as the two men struggled for dominance. Her pounding heart seemed caught in her throat. She'd never seen Alex fight like that before. Determination, purpose and control moved through every block and every blow with a force that took her breath away. But he was fighting cleanly, with a focus on defending himself and humanely bringing Castor to his knees. Castor was bigger, stronger and meaner, a man who fought dirty and was willing to kill without hesitation, as he tried to drive Alex back into the flames.

She'd always known Alex was an athlete and strong. But even when she'd heard he was becoming a bodyguard and even after seeing him disarm Brick, part of her still hadn't imagined that he'd have the discipline and power to fight this way. Or dreamed that he'd need to.

A crack split the frozen air. The balcony above the men's heads caved toward them in a cascade of burning wood. Alex disappeared into the smoke and flames.

A cry slipped from her lips. *Help me, Lord. What do I do?*

Falling snow sizzled against the burning house. She raced back to the snowmobile, landed hard on the seat and slapped her helmet's visor down. Her body slid into the driver's seat. Her hand reached for the handles.

She wouldn't leave him. No matter what, she would not leave Alex alone to die.

"Get off that snowmobile! Now!" a harsh voice barked. For a fraction of a second she was too shocked to move. A second figure, imposing and masked, strode out of the woods. She blinked. Castor? But she'd just seen him fighting Alex in the flames. Then she saw the sneer on his mouth and realized he wasn't the same man she'd left with a bloody lip back at the Rhodeses' cottage. A knife flashed in his hand. "Get down on your knees. Hands up. Now!"

Never. She started the engine. He lunged. His hand grabbed at her body, trying to drag her off the snowmobile with such force that for an instant she almost fell. She swung back, catching his jaw with her elbow. He grunted and slashed at her. The knife sliced through the side of her ski pants, nearly grazing her skin. She gunned the engine. He swung again. The snowmobile shot forward. And she heard the blade of the knife clang against the back of the snowmobile.

She flew forward into the clearing. Thick forest lay to her left with a path she knew

curved back to the lake. The road to the highway lay to her right. But she drove straight
ahead toward the flames. Her eyes stayed
locked on the smoke ahead. *Hold on, Alex. I'm
coming for you.* The falling snow and smoke
were red with flames. She swerved to a stop,
yanked her helmet open and felt the heat sear
her lungs.

"Alex!" She screamed his name with all her
might, praying he'd hear her.

Flaming debris rained down from above
her. How long would it take for the snow
to put out the fire? How much of the forest
would burn before it did? The masked man
with a knife was charging through the trees
after her. Any moment now he would catch
her again, trapping her between him and the
flames.

*Help me, Lord! If I don't leave I could die.
But I can't leave without Alex. I'm his only
hope.*

Then she saw him, running through the
smoke and snow toward her. Relief exploded
like laughter through her lungs. Then she felt
Alex leap onto the snowmobile behind her.
His arms locked around her waist. "Go!"

Bullets thundered from the woods to their
right. Wind licked the flames ahead, sending

the fire straight at them. There was only one way to go. She'd have to risk the lake. She swerved right, driving straight down the hill, dodging between trees and rocks. Branches beat against them. Boulders loomed from the snow. Then they shot out onto the ice, the traction disappeared beneath them and there was nothing but the rush of the engine, the roar of flames and gunfire behind him, and the thick snow smacking their bodies.

They flew, skimming along the ice. The trees and shoreline blurred beside them.

Keep an eye on the shifts in the colors of the ice patterns, follow the channel markers and watch out for the buoys. Alex's words from earlier echoed in her mind. All she had to do was trace the lines of the lake, and they'd eventually reach the safety of his cottage. But where were they? She didn't know this branch of the lake and the channel markers had disappeared under the snow.

Lord, help me. Please help me find a safe place for us to stop. A safe place for us to hide.

Then Alex tapped her shoulder firmly. He grabbed her left arm and pulled it. The snowmobile swerved hard, responding to his touch. Then she felt his other arm come off her waist.

Both of his hands slid on top of her forearms. He guided her arms, steering them from behind. Slight left. Little to the right. Now back to the left. Guiding her motions. Navigating for them as she drove.

Thank you, babe. Alex would never steer her wrong.

They were going to make it.

The snowmobile hit a rock buried under the snow. They lurched forward. The snowmobile caught air. Alex flew off the back. But the hole in her pants leg caught on the machine. The snowmobile flipped, yanking her body along with it. She hit the ice and felt it crack beneath her. The snowmobile began to sink, dragging her with it. In vain she struggled to free herself. Freezing water hit her body, knocking the air from her lungs. She slipped under and thrashed against the snowmobile. Her pants ripped. Her leg tore free. Desperately she broke through the surface and yanked the helmet from her head. Her hands struggled to find something to grasp but the ice broke under her hands.

"Alex! Help!"

Nothing but the whistle of the wind filled her ears.

Alex was gone, and she was going to drown.

* * *

Alex rolled, feeling the ice hit his body like cement. The air was knocked from his lungs. His head smacked the ice sending stars before his eyes. For a moment, he tumbled helplessly, tossed and jostled by the force of gravity even as he heard Theresa's voice cry on the wind and the ugly, unrelenting sound of ice breaking. He braced his arms against the ice and slid to a stop, but even then his head swam so hard he couldn't pull himself to stand up.

Then he heard the sound of her fighting against the water and knew she'd gone under.

"Theresa! Can you hear me?"

God, please, may she be okay.

He forced himself to his feet, blinded for a moment by the thick snow whirling in every direction. Dizziness swept over him. The thought of her being in danger beat hard inside his chest like a war drum.

"Over here!" she called.

"Hold on!" He flew across the ice toward the sound of her voice. "I'm coming!"

"Stop! Wait! It's not safe!"

He slid to a stop, just as he heard the moan and strain of the ice beneath his feet. He dropped to his knees on the frozen lake, frustration building behind his eyes as he fought the sudden impulse to punch the ice in frustration and agony. It was too thin. If he wasn't careful he could fall through, and then they'd both drown. Still, the urge to leap to his feet and tear across the ice toward her was so strong it took all his will not to. He shut his eyes so tightly it hurt. *God, help me think!* He'd taken extensive emergency wilderness survival training. He had all the knowledge he needed to get her out alive. He just had to stay calm. He had to stay focused and maintain self-control, even as he could feel the impulsive, headstrong young man he used to be rearing up inside him.

"Alex?" Theresa's voice broke and he could tell she was treading water. "I'm so scared and I'm so cold. I don't know if I can make it out of the water on my own."

"It's going to be okay." A deeper calm than he'd ever felt before filled his voice. "You won't have to. I'm coming to get you."

He started toward her, crawling slowly on his hands and knees, feeling the creak under him with every movement. He could hear her praying, softly and quietly, as he moved over the ice toward her. Forcing himself to go slowly when he knew she was in danger was agonizing.

"Don't try to pull yourself up," he said. "Just drape your elbows over the edge of the ice, let it balance you, and tread water."

Then through the blowing snow he could see her face—white and terrified. Ice crystals had already started forming on her wet hair. She was hanging over the edge of the ice, one hand clenching her backpack, which she'd somehow managed to get off her back and toss out ahead of her onto the ice.

It took everything inside him not to lunge across the ice and grab her.

"You're going to stay calm, okay?" He unwound the scarf from around his neck. "The biggest enemy we face right now is panic and I need you to be calm for me. Because, believe me, staying calm for you right now is one of the hardest things I've ever had to do."

"It's okay, babe." She nodded. A faint, frightened smile crossed her lips. "I trust you."

That's my baby. Emotion swelled in his heart. There she was, treading water in a frozen lake and still trying to reassure him. "Toss me the backpack. I'll tie my scarf around it and send it back. Then we'll use it to pull you out."

"I'm worried that if I let go of the backpack

I'll go back under." Her teeth chattered. "I'm treading water but I can barely feel my legs."

"Okay, then. I'm coming to you." He crawled closer, inch by inch, feeling the creak and strain of the ice beneath him. Then he felt his hand punch through the ice in front of him. He slid backward to keep from falling through. Several feet of ice-cold water spread between them. Prayers surged through his heart. He knew how dangerous it was to leap into the water to save her and how that would put them both in more danger. But he'd risk it, if he had to. If it was a matter of either jumping into the water or letting her drown it wasn't even a choice.

He'd risk his life for hers every time.

"I'm sorry." Desperation surged through his voice, and his voice almost cracked under the strain of it. "I can't get any closer to you without jumping in."

"Then catch!" She hurled the backpack at him. He lunged for it, barely managed to grab it before it slid into the water. His fingers curled over the strap. *Thank You, God!* He looped the scarf around the handles and tied it tightly.

A faint but courageous smile brushed her

lips. Yet he could see the strain in her eyes. She wouldn't be able to tread water indefinitely.

"I'm going to back up," he said. "Then I'm going to throw it back. I need you to loop your arms through it, so you're wearing it across your chest, and hang on. Okay? I'll pull you out."

"Okay." Her voice was so faint he could barely hear it. He slid backward across the ice. How long was his scarf? Four feet? Five? Whatever it was, it could be the difference between life and death. He dropped to his stomach and lay there, just feet away from her, as she swam toward the edge of the ice. Then he raised the backpack above his head and threw. The backpack flew through the air. "Got it!"

He felt the weight shift as she grabbed it. The scarf stretched and it was all he could do to keep hold of it. He sucked in a painful breath. Okay, now here was the hardest part.

"Take a big kick and get as much of your body up on the edge of the ice as you can. Then I need you to crawl forward."

"Okay." She kicked and launched her body up onto the ice. The ice creaked. Lines of cracking ice spread out around her like cracks on a windshield. Her body slipped back into the water and for a moment she disappeared, before she pushed her way back to the surface.

"Theresa! Go limp! Don't try to climb out. Any move you make could break the ice again."

For a brief second, she glanced up at the snow pelting down and he could see the fear flickering deep inside her eyes. Then her determined gaze met his and his mind flashed back to when he'd found her trapped underneath her capsized sailboat so many years ago. He'd expected her to be panicked. Instead, she'd been so strong and full of faith he'd known in that instant he was going to fall in love with her.

"I trust you," she said.

Her body went limp in the frozen water. It was all on him now.

NINE

He lay on his stomach on the ice and felt her full weight pull back against the scarf. Alex gritted his teeth and pulled as hard as he could. His arms strained. His muscles ached. For a moment he felt the scarf slipping in his grasp and thought it was going to tear. Then he heard a gasp leave her lips as her body slid out onto the ice.

"Thank You, God."

"Amen." He pulled her body toward him across the ice. Slowly she came closer, until finally her fingers touched his. He dropped the scarf. He grabbed her hands and squeezed them as hard as he dared. She squeezed him back. He crawled backward, keeping one of her hands clenched tightly in his, until he was confident they were close enough to shore. Then he stood, carefully took the backpack and slid it over his shoulders. "Can you stand?"

"I think so," she said. He helped her to her feet. She took one step and fell against him. Tears caught in her voice even as she struggled to smile. "Maybe not."

"It's okay. I've got you." He looped one hand under her knees and the other under her shoulders. She slid her arms around his neck. He lifted her up into his arms and cradled her against his chest. The movement was so instinctual, it was as if she'd always been there. His throat felt tight. "The biggest danger right now is the cold. We don't want hypothermia to set in. We've got to get you somewhere warm, and fast."

She didn't answer. Her head fell into the crook of his neck. He pulled her tighter into his arms and looked up at the steep snow bank ahead of him. Thick woods filled his view. He ran up the hill. The sky grew darker. His legs sank deep into the snow. He stumbled over hidden rocks and buried roots. Branches pressed against them. He felt Theresa's body shudder against his. Then her arms slipped off his neck.

"Hey, Theresa. You stay awake for me. Okay?" He tilted her face toward him. He brushed his lips against her cheek. It was as cold as ice. She murmured something softly.

He held her tighter. His mouth brushed hers, feeling for the heat of her breath. Then her arms slid up around his neck again and he felt her kiss him back. The kiss deepened as he cradled her body against him, like two survivors clinging to each other for warmth and life.

Then she pulled back, her eyes fluttered open and he realized with a jolt that he'd just kissed her.

"Hey, you just focus on staying awake and alive for me, okay?" he said. His voice choked in his throat. "Hold on to me tight. I need you to stay with me."

His eyes scanned the trees as the blowing snow whitewashed the world around him into a series of unfamiliar shapes. He clenched his jaw, turned right, and followed the shoreline, praying with every step he'd see something he recognized.

He could feel Theresa's grip slipping again. Her body was growing limp in his arms. How much longer could they survive? How much longer could she make it? Desperation battled with determination inside Alex's core. *God, please help me save her.*

He stumbled out of the trees, tripped and nearly fell onto a set of steps buried beneath the snow. He'd found a path. He turned and followed it up through the trees. A building loomed ahead of him. He ploughed on. He ran up a flight of wooden steps and onto a porch. He shifted Theresa's weight just enough to grab the door handle and, when it didn't turn, kicked the door hard enough to break the flimsy lock. The door swung open. *Thank You, God.* They stumbled out of the snow and into the gloom of a huge open-concept cottage. Ceiling beams arched high above his head.

The Cedar Lake community was so tight-knit he had no doubt he'd be forgiven by the owner even before he apologized. For now, he wasn't sure whose cottage this was. He set down Theresa down gently on a thick fur rug in front of a huge stone fireplace.

"Thank you." Her voice slipped out, barely more than a whisper.

He grabbed an armful of blankets and quilts off the sofa and quickly draped them around her. Then he knelt, eased her gloves off her hands and took both her hands in his. He raised them to his lips, kissed her cold skin and then gently massaged the feeling back into them. They warmed under his touch. "Can you wiggle your toes?"

"Yes, my boots are pretty waterproof. So are my gloves."

Her voice seemed to grow stronger with every word. "The only place water really seeped in was the hole in my ski pants. The rest of me is more damp than soaked."

"You should still change out of those clothes as soon as you can. I'll search the bedrooms for something for you to change into."

"I've got a change of clothes in the backpack," she said, and there was something so very practical and obvious about her saying it that he almost laughed. "There's food, too, and fire-starting papers. Duct tape, too, which I can use to patch up my ski pants. The backpack is waterproof and everything inside is all in waterproof pouches, so it all should still be dry. I hope."

He shrugged the backpack off his shoulders, thankful she'd had the tenacity and quick thinking to grab it when they'd left the Rhodeses' cottage. She was incredible. He felt for her boots under the mound of blankets and helped her untie the laces. "Okay, once you're ready I'll make us a fire. Then we can regroup and hopefully figure out where we are."

"I know where we are. Some of Paul Wright's relatives bought it. The kitchen and study walls have been knocked out, but the overall bones are still the same." Her eyes rose to the ceiling above. "This used to be my cottage."

Twenty minutes later she was standing in the entranceway of what used to be her downstairs bedroom, changed into clean dry clothes, watching as Alex knelt before the fireplace coaxing a flame to life. The backpack had kept the T-shirt, yoga pants and socks in her backpack dry. Her heavy-duty waterproof gloves and boots had kept her fingers and toes from freezing. They were safe. They were warm. There was so much to be thankful for. Yet, as she stood in the doorway of the room that was once hers, looking out across the room at the man she'd once loved, the weight of everything she'd lost was so much she was almost crushed by it.

This was the room she'd planned to get dressed for her wedding in. Her mother had bought a special, antique full-length mirror and a vanity for the occasion. Her father had installed a special hook on the back of the door for her wedding dress. Her beautifully carved wooden hope chest, which had lived at the end of her bed at home for as long as she could remember, had been brought up weeks before the wedding and sat in the corner of the room. Her mother had already started filling it with early wedding gifts and cards.

Theresa leaned against the doorframe. Sure, the new owners had made some changes and renovations. She couldn't blame Alex for not recognizing it at first. Her bed, vanity, hope chest and mirror were long gone, presumably sold in the bankruptcy auction, like so much else in her childhood. But if she closed her eyes she could almost see the room as it once was. She could still remember the delicate smell of her wedding dress, fresh from a final cleaning and fitting, the gentle rustle of it as her door had opened and closed, and the softness of the fabric beneath her fingers.

"Hey, you okay?" Alex's voice snapped her back into the present. "Is there anything I can help you with?"

He was kneeling before the fire on one knee, a silhouette, ringed by the golden light of the fire, like the shadow of a past she'd lost long ago. He'd shed his winter gear, too. Blue jeans and a simple long-sleeved T-shirt outlined his strong form. He'd somehow managed to keep every bit of the lithe form of his youth while adding to it the strength and confidence of manhood.

An unexpected flush rose to her cheeks as she remembered the spontaneous kiss they'd shared outside in the snow.

"I'm fine. Thank you." She scooped her wet, cold and soggy clothes up into her arms.

"Good." A charming, boyish grin crossed his face, sending the warmth from her face spreading down over her chest and setting off sparklers in her heart. "I was worried for a moment that I'd lost you."

She crossed the dark floor toward him. People said that places tended to seem smaller when you revisited them as adults. But, in that moment, it was as if the room lengthened and stretched with every step she took. Alex seemed close and yet so far away, as if she were walking through a dream and if she stepped too close he'd disappear.

"I figured we'd warm up, get something to eat and make a plan," Alex said. "The electricity's not working, the phone's dead and I couldn't pick up a signal on either my cell phone or the CB radio. But we can boil some water on the fire and make up some of the dried soup you packed. I don't see anything that resembles a trunk here either, but it doesn't look like Castor and his crew have tossed this place. I vote we rest here for a bit, wait for the snow to die down and then continue to my cottage on foot. Hopefully the Wrights have skis or snowshoes or even a snowmobile I just haven't found yet. Do you know which part of the Wright family bought it?"

"Paul's aunt and uncle, I think. But it was years ago."

She frowned. She didn't know who now slept in the room that was once hers, who stared up at the ceiling she'd once stared at, or if they knew every creak of the floorboards like she once had. This cottage was no longer her favorite place in the world. Just like the man kneeling in front of the fireplace was no longer the man she was going to spend the rest of her life with. Just like the heavy mid-February snowstorm that was wreaking havoc on the lake when people should be looking forward to spring, everything was different from how it should be.

"I'm hoping that Castor will wait out the storm, as well, and resume his search for whatever he's looking for once the snow dies down." Alex frowned. "I'm sorry. I owe you an apology about the safe house. I had no idea we'd be ambushed."

"No, you don't need to apologize." Theresa dropped to her knees on the rug beside him. She set the wet clothes beside her on the floor. "You made the best decision you could. You had no idea that it could be a trap. As for my hunch about following the markings I'd seen in the car, well, they'd have sent us straight to the rocks in front of this cottage. Maybe even the same rocks I crashed the snowmobile on. And it's pretty clear Zoe and Mandy aren't here either. I don't think it needs to be a competition about who's the most wrong."

"Thank you," he said, with a mild smile. "But we still have no idea who Castor is, how he knew where we'd be heading, or what he's looking for and is seemingly willing to kill indiscriminately for. We also still don't know where the police are. I'm certain that Daniel called them after I contacted him about Castor and his goons attacking you at the Rhodeses' cottage, and the longer we go without seeing any sign of the authorities, the more worried I am." Concern tinged the depths of his blue eyes. "We still don't know where Zoe and Mandy are."

Guilt stabbed her heart. He was in pain.

The situation was terrifying. Their lives had both been threatened. Now was no time to allow the attraction to him that still nipped at the edges of her heart to take hold or let herself think about what might have been.

She stood, scooped the wet clothes back up again and turned her attention to the fireplace. The new mantel was huge, and the Wrights had covered the old brick with stone. Still, the rest of the cavernous fireplace she'd spent countless nights curled up in front of was the same comforting shape and size it had always been. She slung her jeans and T-shirt over the far end of the mantel, then reached to hang the sweatshirt. Her shin smacked hard against something sharp. She tripped and nearly cried out in pain. The clothes slipped from her hand. A heavy, old-fashioned poker and broom sat on the edge of the fireplace and she'd just smashed her shin right into it.

"What happened?" In an instant, Alex had leaped to her side. He scooped the wet sweatshirt up from the floor.

Heat rose to her cheeks. She rolled up her pants leg. Already she could see the red welt of a bruise forming. "I just hadn't expected that to be there."

Alex nodded. She watched as he hung

the sweatshirt out across the mantel in front of the fire and felt the flush in her cheeks burn hotter. An odd tension spread across his shoulders. He knew it was one of his old sweatshirts. She knew it, too. They'd both known all this time and neither of them had said anything about it. Yet there it was, hanging in front of them. Like a reminder of everything they'd lost and everything they still weren't able to talk about.

Without even thinking she took a step back and sat, expecting to drop onto the comforting softness of the couch. Instead, the back of her thighs hit the hard edge of an unfamiliar wood-edged chair, sending her tumbling onto the nest of blankets still lying on the floor. She could feel laughter bubbling out from the back of her throat, even as tears of frustration tumbled from her eyes. The whole situation was crazy. She was stuck in the cottage that used to be hers, with the man whose heart she'd once thought was hers, in a storm that none of the forecasters had managed to see coming.

"I expected my old couch to be there." She wiped her hand over her eyes, brushing away tears that could have been from frustration or laughter, she couldn't tell. "Just like I didn't expect that brush and poker to be where my shin wanted to go. It feels like I've fallen down the rabbit hole and into some alternate universe…"

Her voice trailed off. Alex sat down on the carpet beside her. He pushed the blankets aside in a casual, languid way that looked like he wasn't even thinking about where they were going, and yet somehow still managed to drape them over her legs. His shoulder bumped lightly against hers, as if his arm couldn't decide whether it wanted to wrap around her. Everything inside her wanted to nestle into his side. Neither of them moved closer.

"You said this whole thing felt like looking into some other, alternative reality?" Alex said. "I know that feeling. When that screen opened up on my computer and I saw you sitting there, in my old sweatshirt…" His voice trailed off. He chuckled. "For a second, I didn't know what to think."

"Sorry. I was cold. Zoe grabbed it from a drawer at your cottage and threw it at me. I slipped it on without thinking."

"It's okay," he said softly. "I didn't say I minded."

His shoulder bumped against hers again.

She looked up. His face was so close she could see the deep gray line circling the blue of his eyes. "Honestly, I hadn't seen it in years. I stormed home the day we broke up. I haven't been back up here since. Not until today. I couldn't handle the memories."

Firelight flickered on his face, outlining the strong lines of his jaw. There was something so intense in the depths of his gaze that she bit her lip and had to look away.

Something she'd told her therapy clients time and again tripped across her mind. *Sometimes the hardest thing to get over is something you never had to begin with.* When relationships were damaged and broken beyond repair, when people died, and when dreams were dashed, those left wounded didn't just grieve for what they'd lost. They cried for the life they'd hoped for but would never get to have. They mourned the graduations, weddings, anniversaries and celebrations that would never happen. They hurt over the close relationship with a sibling, spouse, parent or child they'd never experience. Despite the number of times she'd told people this, and how well her brain had internalized it as truth, somehow she'd never felt the full sting of it until right then, in that moment, sitting in front of the fire beside Alex.

Pain welled up inside her, pushing tears to the corners of her eyes. Their hands shouldn't be inches away but not touching. They should be holding hands. There should be wedding rings on their fingers. They should have children, a home and a cottage of their own. They should be looking forward to celebrating their nine-year anniversary in August, instead of sitting there in awkward silence like strangers. The life they should've lived had somehow been broken and lost, and there was no way to get it back. She buried her face in her hands and blinked back the tears before they could fall.

Alex's hand slipped onto her shoulder. He rubbed her back gently in between her shoulder blades.

"I'm sorry I wasn't there for you," he said. "When your parents lost their business and you lost your home, I should've been there. I should've stood by you and been the kind of friend you deserved."

She felt his hand slide up the side of her neck. His fingers ran slowly through her hair, then brushed along the side of her face. Her head fell against his shoulder, and she felt his lips brush over the top of her head. Then she tilted her head up toward his and his mouth found hers again with a sweet, simple kiss that reminded her of how young they'd both once been and all the possibilities that had spread out before them. Then he wrapped both arms around her and pulled her into a hug. She pressed her face against the soft, warm fabric of his shirt. If only she could stay here in that moment, with her eyes closed and the fire burning. If only she could let herself pretend, just for a moment, that they were still the people they used to be and that everything they'd had hadn't really been lost.

"I just wish you hadn't pushed me away like that," he murmured. "I was so hurt by how you ended things and broke our engagement, the only thing I knew how to do was withdraw and disappear."

"What?" She opened her eyes and pulled back out of his arms. "What are you talking about? I didn't push you away, and I definitely didn't break up with you."

"Yes, with all due respect, you did," he said. Something firm moved over the softness that had been in his eyes just moments before. "You told me your parents had decided to cancel parts of the wedding and then you nagged me about not having a job."

"Because a twenty-one-year-old man who's about to be married should have a job!" Her voice rose. "It was one thing to get married when you had a full scholarship that included an internship and campus accommodation. It was a whole other thing when you dropped all that on a whim and expected we'd just figure things out as we went along. My parents couldn't afford the wedding we had planned. They had no way to pay for it. You're the one who demanded I give you the ring back."

"Because you didn't give me any other choice!" He ran his hand over his head, like he couldn't actually believe the words was hearing. "You knew I was miserable in that program. You knew I wanted to quit. It wasn't on a whim. But you kept insisting I stick it out. Don't you get it? You were the most important thing in my world back then—the only important thing in my world—and rather than trying to understand where I was coming from, you just stood there, criticizing me and berating me and making me feel like I was worthless. You made me feel like I wasn't good enough for you because I didn't have a real job or enough money saved up in the bank."

She stood up. He stood, too.

No, she hadn't told him any of that. She couldn't have. Could she? Because that's not what she remembered feeling. She'd been scared and worried for her future. She'd been upset he'd quit another university program. But she'd still loved him. She'd still wanted to marry him. How could they be remembering the past so differently?

"You ran," she said. Her head shook. "Things got tough between us and you ran. Like you always do. You got one glimpse of how hard real grown-up life and marriage was going to be and you bailed."

"I didn't bail on you. I was pushed," he said. "I just wish you'd have let me step up and be there for you. I wish you'd have let me help!"

"Let you?" Her voice rose. "What was stopping you? You could've come to the bankruptcy auction and held my hand, or followed me when I ran off crying because it was all too much for me to handle. You could've doubled down on your desire to marry me and stubbornly insisted we were still going to get married and that you'd help me find a way to make it work. You could've taken charge, instead of counting on me to sort everything out. Or, at least, you could've helped share the load."

"Like you'd have ever trusted me to take charge of anything." He threw his hands up in the air. "Don't you remember what you were like? You had to be in control of everything. You were particular. You got so anxious and worried if things didn't work out just the way you wanted them to. You were such a—"

His voice cut off suddenly, with a grimace, like the taste of the words that he was about to speak tasted rotten on his tongue.

"'Such a finicky little princess,'" she said. "That's what you were going to say, right?"

"No." He met her gaze, full-on and unflinching. "I was going to say, such a frightened young woman who didn't know how to let me love her."

Her lips shook. No, she hadn't been that at all, had she? It'd all been his fault for running away. Hadn't it?

"Well, if you'd loved me, you should've fought for me."

"Yeah, you're right. I should've." He took a step toward her. Tension crackled between them like sparks in the fire. "But I didn't know how to, and neither did you."

"Break, break. Hello?" A voice crackled

through the CB radio, female and frightened. "Anybody there? I think something bad is happening, and I don't know what to do."

TEN

Theresa spun around, searching for the source of the sound. But Alex got to the radio first. He snatched it up from the table by the wall.

"Hi! I mean, come in," Alex said. There was a long pause on the other end. Then he added, "Over?"

"Are you with the police?" the young voice continued, in that very serious tone a child puts on when they're trying to hide the fact that they're frightened. "I need to talk to the police. Over."

Theresa's hand touched his arm and whispered. "Remember, she's only a child."

Alex paused. Then he handed the radio to Theresa and whispered, "You talk to her this time."

Theresa took the radio.

"Copy that," Theresa said softly. "I'm sorry,

we're not the police. Do you have a telephone? You need to call nine-one-one. Over."

The girl sniffed and, to Theresa's relief, it sounded more frustrated than scared.

"I called nine-one-one before. But they yelled at me for being 'a stupid kid making a crank call' and said, 'they were tired of pranks like mine when there are real emergencies out there.'" There was a pause. "I'm not a little kid by the way. I'm turning nine in April."

"Ah. That must've been frustrating." Theresa sat down on the edge of the couch, feeling an invisible psychotherapist cloak slide over her shoulders like a mantle. She'd counseled so many kids in her line of work, kids who'd learned at a young age just how hard life could be. "My name's Theresa. I want to listen to you and see if I can help you. This is Bee, right? You talked to my friend Alex before. Can I call you Bee?"

"No, you can't. Only my daddy calls me Bee."

Alex stifled a snort. Theresa smiled. "How about April then? Because your birthday's in April."

The voice paused a moment. "Okay. I guess that's okay."

"Why do you need to call the police, April? Are you hurt? Are you in danger?"

"No. I'm okay. I'm in my grandpa's house. He's outside trying to shovel or something so my daddy's able to get in the driveway when he gets home. He drives a truck. He should've been here a long time ago. Sometimes daddy and I talk on the radio, for fun. He taught me radio voice procedure words, but I don't always remember to use them."

"That's okay," Theresa said. "We don't know them very well, either."

"Daddy's not answering his radio. The roads are bad and there's lots of accidents." Her voice dropped. "I'm not supposed to be on the radio when there are storms and accidents."

Alex coughed. Theresa looked up. His fingers spun in a speed-it-up motion. She shot him a warning glance and slid her palm over the speaker.

"She's not answering your questions," he hissed.

"Yeah, I got that. She's a kid. Kids don't always get to the point, especially when they're scared. Now let me do my job." She turned her back to him. "I can understand why your grandpa doesn't want you on the radio when there are a lot of accidents. Are you listening to hear if your daddy's truck is safe?"

"Uh-huh." April sniffed.

"I'll pray your daddy gets home safe. I'm looking for two of my friends. I think they're lost, too. Their names are Zoe and Mandy. Have you heard them on the radio?"

"No," April said. "But I keep hearing angry men shouting. Using a lot of really bad words."

"That sounds scary and confusing."

"I'm almost nine," April said, again. "I've heard lots of bad words before. Grandpa and Daddy just don't let me say them."

Theresa stifled a smile. "Well, you sound very smart and they sound like they love you very much."

"The angry men at Cedar Lake said they were going to kill someone if they didn't find some box. Well, one of them said he was going to kill someone."

"How many angry men were there?"

"Two. I think. I'm not sure."

"Now, I need you to think really hard, April. Did they mention any names? Or who they were going to kill?"

There was a long pause. "*Tanner* is a name, right?"

Theresa's eyes met Alex's. *Tanner Mullock.*

"Yes, April. That's a name."

"I told Grandpa about the angry men and we called the police together," she said. "I talked to them, too, because I'd heard the stuff on the radio. But the police said they'd already received one hoax call about trouble out there tonight and if people didn't stop making prank calls they'd throw us in jail."

Theresa felt her jaw drop. Alex's eyebrows rose and she could see the frustration and worry filling his eyes. Had police dismissed the call his boss had placed about her being attacked? But why? Surely if they'd done their jobs and made their way to Mandy Rhodes's cottage they'd have found it destroyed and also Brick's body.

"Grandpa said the police were really stupid sometimes and went outside to shovel the snow," April added. "I don't think the police understood the part about Tanner being a name."

It didn't sound like the police had taken April's grandfather seriously. But it was hard to know what exactly he'd told them. What was more worrying was the idea that Daniel had called in a very serious crime and they hadn't taken it seriously.

"Hi, April, my name's Alex." He knelt

down beside the radio. "I was a bit rude to you before. I'm sorry about that."

"It's okay," April said grudgingly. "Are you friends with Theresa?"

"Really good friends," Alex said. "She's a really good person to talk to when you're scared or upset about something. I probably should've let her talk to you before." His eyes flickered over her face, and warmth spread down her limbs. "Now I need you to be really brave and listen, okay, April? My little sister, Zoe, is one of the women that's missing. I'm really worried for her. The police need to know about her and Mandy. I'm sorry the police were mean to you. Adults aren't always good listeners. My friend Corey got in trouble with the police when I was younger, and I think that was really hard for him. But my best friend Joshua's dad is a really good police officer. I need you to get your grandpa to try and call my boss Daniel and give him a message for me. Can you try and do that?"

There was a long pause, and for a moment Theresa feared they'd lost her. Alex's hand slipped over hers and squeezed.

"I'm going to go get Grandpa, okay?"

The radio went to static. Theresa looked at Alex. He was still holding her hand.

"What do you think it means that Castor mentioned Tanner Mullock's name?" she asked.

There was crash outside, like a heavy tree branch had broken off from the storm and toppled to the ground. He dropped her hand and leaped to his feet.

"Stay here," he said. "I'm going to check that out. Hopefully it's nothing, but I don't want to risk it."

"If April gets her grandfather, give him Daniel's phone number and a quick rundown of what's happening," Alex said. He shoved his feet into boots. "He doesn't have to call the police if he doesn't want to. He can just call Daniel. But remember, as long as we're on an open channel, other people can listen in so don't say anything that could compromise our safety or give away our position." He started for the door. "And if you hear anything that sounds like trouble, find something to protect yourself with and hide."

"Stay safe," Theresa said. "Please. Don't do anything crazy. If there's danger, don't rush into it and try to be a hero."

He turned back. She was standing in front of the fire, just three steps away from him.

More care than he'd ever hoped to see glimmered in the depths of her green eyes.

But it was clear now that she'd never understood why he'd walked away from her all those years ago. And she still saw him as that rash, foolhardy, irresponsible kid he'd been a long time ago. He shouldn't have kissed her. Twice now he'd allowed himself to get caught up in his emotions and let his heart overrule his brain. He couldn't let that happen again.

"Being a hero is kind of my job now." A wry smile turned at the corner of his lips. "It's what I've trained for and prepared for in the almost two years it took to build Ash Private Security. You did an amazing job talking to April. You're clearly a great psychotherapist. Now, I've got to go do my job, too. And I need you to stay safe, stay out of the way and try to get a message out through April's grandfather."

"Okay." The smile dropped from her lips.

"Thank you. Now, hopefully that noise was nothing but some falling ice. But I need to make sure. I'll be right back."

Then, without letting himself look back, he grabbed a ski mask from a basket of winter gear by the door, yanked it down his head and stepped out into the falling snow. The evening sky had grown dark behind the clouds. Snow lashed down, blurring his vision and making the ground slick beneath his feet. His eyes scanned the darkness, waiting for some kind of sound or motion to let him know which way to go. Carefully he paced along the side of the cottage then back again. Nothing.

He paused at the cottage doorway and glanced in, fighting the urge to go back inside. Theresa now knelt by the fire. Golden firelight illuminated her skin. Her long hair shone dark bronze. She was the most beautiful thing he'd ever seen in his life. He swallowed hard. If he was honest, maybe she'd never been a true partner in his eyes. Instead, she'd been a trophy to be won, back at the time he'd collected trophies with ease. She'd been the one, shiny, perfect thing he'd wanted by his side, through thick and thin, because he'd loved her and needed her with the shallow emotions of a youth who hadn't yet learned how to stand on his own two feet and whose loyalty and strength had never been tested.

Now, here he was, just a couple of years into a job at a new company, paying off the debts of his past mistakes and bunking with his sister on Daniel's country property. He owned no land, had invested most of his savings in his bodyguard training and had no career stability. He might be almost thirty, but he was no closer to giving Theresa the life she deserved, let alone the kind of life that had once been ripped out from under her. Now it was time he let the dream of her go.

A light flickered to his right, off and on so quickly he wondered for a moment if his eyes were playing tricks on him. He headed toward it. For a long moment he walked blindly, the snow heavy under his feet, seeing nothing but shades of white and gray. Thick, blowing snow stung his skin. He rolled the ski mask down over his face. Then came another flicker of yellow light, lighting up the snow.

He stumbled down the hill until he reached a small two-story building, half-hidden in the woods. It was too big to be a shed and too small to be a cottage. He felt along the aluminum siding and to find a door. It was ajar. He paused with his hand on the doorframe and listened. Silence. Was this another trap? And if so, what was he going to do about it? If one of Castor's men, or somebody else who was after this trunk, was hiding out this close to where Theresa now sat, curled up by the fire, then Alex couldn't sit back and ignore the potential threat, even if it meant risking his own life in the process.

He whispered a prayer for strength, speed and, above all, wisdom. Then, slowly and carefully, he slipped inside. Shadowy shapes came into focus before his eyes in the dim light. There was a knee-high table with four small chairs, a cabinet lined with wooden animals and a long box along the wall. A narrow ladder led up to a hole in the floor above. Small puddles of melting snow glimmered on the ground.

Somebody had been here. Maybe they still were. He had to draw them out and make them fight on his terms, not theirs. He was done with walking into traps.

In one quick, seamless motion he snatched up a handful of snow and threw it at the shadow in the corner of the room. The shadows shifted. A feminine figure dashed across the floor toward the ladder. A sudden bright light flashed in his eyes, blinding him. Alex raised his hands to strike.

ELEVEN

Shielding his eyes, Alex leaped toward the blinding light and aimed a decisive blow across the jaw of the figure behind it. But his blow never landed. The flashlight clattered onto the floor and rolled, sending wild shadows flying around the wooden space. The figure jumped two steps up onto the ladder, just long enough to dodge his fist, then launched at him. A quick one-two of sharp fists struck his stomach with punches that nearly knocked the air from his lungs and would have taken a lesser man to the floor.

Then she leaped back. Her hands rose steadily in front of her, ready to fight.

He didn't need the light to know that fighting stance. Relief exploded in his heart. "Zoe!"

"Oh, wow, Alex?" His sister's voice rushed out in a whisper. "Really? It's you?"

"Yeah, it's really me." He yanked off the ski mask. His tiny sister launched herself at him in a hug. *Thank You, God!* His sister was safe. "Where's Mandy?"

"Upstairs." She hugged him so hard he felt it in his ribs. Then she stepped back. "This place has an attic with bunks. We were going to wait out the storm here and then try to get to Theresa."

"Theresa's with me," he said. "She's in the Wrights' cottage. We let ourselves in. I heard a crack that sounded like falling ice, came outside to check on it and saw the flashlight flickering."

Zoe whispered a prayer of relief.

"The flashlight was me," she said. "I heard the ice falling, too. The storm's taking out a lot of tree branches."

She climbed up the ladder a few steps and stuck her head through the hole in the floor. "Mandy? Alex and Theresa are here."

He didn't hear an answer. Then Zoe leaped back down.

"She's passed out cold, asleep," she said. "She's exhausted. Mandy didn't sleep at all last night, she just kept pacing. Then there was the car crash and we had to run here through the snow on foot. The Wrights built this place as a bunkhouse for their kids last summer. I just can't believe you got my message to come here. It was a real wild shot."

Her message.

"You scratched letters with your knife in the car?" He hazarded a guess, even though his gut told him what she was about to say.

Zoe nodded. "Yes. After I took Mandy into town, I drove past the road that led to the emergency meeting point, saw tire tracks and knew it was compromised. I was heading back to meet up with Theresa, when some nut job ran me off the road. I heard gunfire and had about two seconds to figure out where to go and how to send Theresa a message."

"You did well," he said. "Theresa figured it out."

"I hoped she'd just stay put at Mandy's family cottage until I was able to reach her," Zoe said. "Honestly, I have no idea what's going on."

"The Rhodeses' cottage has been compromised," he said. "Some masked men have been going from cottage to cottage, ransacking them looking for some kind of trunk they're willing to kill and kidnap for."

Zoe's eyebrows rose. Alex paused. Theresa would be back at the cottage, alone, wondering where he was. But he'd just reunited with Zoe. Their client was safely asleep upstairs. The snow was coming down so fiercely it made driving fairly impossible and walking pretty close to it, providing a short-term protective barrier against Castor. It was the first moment since he'd seen Castor break down the door and charge at Theresa, through the window of a laptop screen, when he didn't feel he was running and battling against the criminals turning the lake he'd grown up loving into a battle zone.

He leaned against the child's table. "Okay, I want to have a really fast five-minute strategy chat before we join Theresa. Okay?"

Zoe's eyes opened wide. But she nodded and sat down beside him. He caught her up in quick, bullet-point form on everything that had happened, from the first attack and the death of Brick, to the damage at the Pattersons' cottage, to finding Howler's body in the crashed car and Gnat holding Theresa at gunpoint, to the explosion at the safe house and finally crashing the snowmobile through the ice. Everything but the two spontaneous kisses he'd shared with the woman he'd once given his youthful heart to and from whom his adult mind knew he was in no position to ask anything in return.

When he was done, Zoe just let out a long breath. "Wow."

"I know." He crossed his long legs at the ankles. "I'm pretty sure that whoever these guys are, they didn't expect to be running into any other people up here this weekend and thought they could just ransack, grab and go. We threw a pretty big wrench in their gears."

"Is it possible that Theresa is their target?" Zoe asked. "You mentioned that two of the men tried to force her to help them search for the trunk. Plus it sounded like Castor was tormenting her pretty specifically. Is it possible she actually does know something about the trunk?"

"Possibly." Alex leaned back. The table creaked beneath him. "Certainly the criminals seem to think that she does. But for now Theresa is as in the dark about what this trunk is or what it contains as I am. Neither of us have been up here in eight and a half years. Theresa's convinced that Castor, or one of his men, has a connection to Cedar Lake.

"I know Corey Patterson had some trouble with the law for drug dealing when he was younger," he added. "It's entirely possible his life went downhill from there and he has deadbeat friends he met in jail who he could convince to help ransack cottages. He could've hidden money or drug paraphernalia up here recently. Theresa mentioned Paul Wright, too, mostly because he's the same age as these guys. But honestly, the person I'm most suspicious about right now is Tanner Mullock. April, the little girl Theresa was talking to on the radio, said something about Castor or somebody else threatening to kill him. Which could mean he's one of the guys Castor brought up here. Or Tanner could be Castor, and April overheard somebody else threating to kill him and blowing his cover."

"Castor can't be Tanner," Zoe said. "He was in a really bad car accident in Toronto about a week ago. His car spun out on the ice. He ended up in the hospital with some kind of internal injury and needed a lot stitches. He had to move back in with his grandparents while he recovers. He'll be on bed rest for weeks. I can't imagine him having the strength to ransack a cottage. Mandy's mom pulled me aside and mentioned it as I was heading out the door, sort of as a reminder to be extracareful."

Considering how overprotective Mandy's parents were, hearing somebody else's kid had spun out was exactly the kind of thing likely to kick their fear into overdrive.

"Then once we get a connection to the outside world we call the Mullocks and see what we can get Tanner to tell us about all this," Alex said. "Also wouldn't hurt for Daniel to get them some extra security. Tanner could be Castor's next target."

There was the soft thud of another branch or hunk of ice falling into the thick snow outside. Now that he'd found Zoe, he was in no hurry for the storm to end. They could all hunker down in the cottage overnight and figure out how to get to his truck back at their cottage and escape the lake in the morning. He just hoped the truck was still there, and that they wouldn't run into Castor and his men.

"In the meantime, Tanner's out as a Castor suspect, and we can add the fact that April heard his name to the big list of things we can't currently understand." Alex ran his hand over his chin. Like why Castor would kill his henchmen, why Castor hadn't searched the Rhodeses' cold cellar for Theresa and why Gnat thought Theresa knew something about the trunk. "It doesn't help that every time someone mentions this infernal trunk all I can imagine is some pirate's chest filled with sparkling doubloons."

"My first thought was that it could either be a dress-up trunk," Zoe said, "or one of those garish things filled with cheap plastic toys in restaurants."

"Which nobody would either kill for or hire thugs to find. My first guess was some kind of war medals or something military-related that Josh's grandfather had passed down to Mandy's side of the family. But that's a stretch now that at least two people have died over this. Obviously drugs, weapons and money are the three main things that criminals kill each other over."

"It could also contain the deed to a property," Zoe suggested. "Or something antique, like coins or jewelry. Old toys or comic books can be really valuable. Or even a diary that contained important information."

He hadn't thought of any of those.

"All good ideas," he said. "But why would anyone keep that in a trunk at Cedar Lake?"

"I have no idea," she said. "The idea is so crazy that I'm tempted to believe Castor is searching for something else entirely and made up the whole story about the trunk to hide his real agenda. Why would he think that Theresa knows something about it? And again, why would it be at a cottage?"

His eyes slid to the long box in the corner of the room. She rolled her eyes.

"I've already checked it," she said. "It's just beach toys. There are more toys and some blankets upstairs."

The question of the trunk sat between them in the dark air of the children's bunkhouse. He checked his watch. He'd been gone almost twenty minutes. "I should get back. Theresa is probably wondering what happened to me."

"I'm sorry I didn't tell you about Theresa being up here with me," Zoe said. "I didn't mean to hide anything important from you. Obviously, Daniel knew. But we never imagined there'd be a reason for you two to ever run into each other."

"It's okay." He squeezed his sister's shoulder. "I know our deal. I didn't want to talk about it, but you and Daniel both thought she was great at what she did, so we agreed that when you consulted with her you'd keep me out of the loop. I can see now that you weren't wrong about her. And nobody could've predicted any of this happening."

He ran his hand over the back of his neck. Zoe nodded.

"I didn't know her parents had declared bankruptcy and lost their cottage," he said. "Let alone that they lost their business and their house. Zoe, how did I possibly miss that? How could I have been so blind? You know her dad loaned me the money for the engagement ring? And I just threw it on the floor in the boathouse in anger without even thinking of repaying him for his kindness. I had no clue there'd been a bankruptcy auction. Where was my head at, that I missed all that happening?"

"I thought you knew." She shrugged. "Guess we all figured she'd told you. The bankruptcy auction was Labor Day weekend in September. You were grieving pretty hard and really angry, too. You'd put us all under strict orders to never mention Theresa's name ever again. My understanding is the Pattersons bought most of the company assets. The Wrights bought the cottage. A bunch of strangers got the furniture. Dad and Mom went. Josh went with his dad. I didn't go. I was pretty mean to her back then, to be honest. I was every bit as mad at her as you were, and thought I'd never forgive her for your breakup. It was just a big, sad, terrible mess. I don't think anybody knew what to say or do about it."

"Including me," he said. He stood up.

His sister's hand brushed his elbow. "But are you okay seeing her now?"

"I'm exhausted, in pain, overwhelmed and shaken up. But that's due to the circumstances. None of that is her fault."

"Understood. I'm going to go wake Mandy." Zoe crossed the room behind him.

He stood in the doorway and stared out at the snow, with half of his heart pulling him toward the cottage where he knew Theresa was and the other half wanting to stay out in the tiny, cold bunkhouse until he knew what to do.

For a moment he'd thought Zoe was about to ask if he still had feelings for Theresa.

He did. He just couldn't let himself think about them. It's not like he was in any position to do anything about it.

"Alex, we've got a problem." Zoe's voice came from behind him. "Mandy managed to get an upstairs window open. She's gone."

Static hissed down the radio line mingling with the crackle of the flames in the fireplace. Theresa's eyes rose to the clock on the wall. It has been over twenty minutes since Alex had stepped out into the storm and more that

that since April has disappeared off the radio. Outside the snow kept growing heavier. The sky kept growing darker.

The door swung open. Theresa leaped to her feet.

"Alex! I'm so glad you're back, I was beginning to worry—"

The words froze on her lips as a slender woman with tumbling blond hair and a red ski jacket stepped through the doorway. Mandy crossed the threshold and stood on the welcome mat, her limbs shaking like an anxious greyhound. *What is she doing here?* Instinctively, Theresa's empty hand stretched out toward her. "Mandy! Wow, am I relieved to see you. How did you get here? Where's Zoe?"

Mandy didn't answer. Her eyes darted around the room. "You alone?"

"Yes, I was with Zoe's brother, Alex, but he went out to investigate a noise." Theresa set the radio down on the couch and crossed the room. "I can't begin to tell you how amazing it is to see you."

"Stop right there. Please." Mandy's voice shook. "Don't come any closer."

"Mandy?" Theresa froze. "Is everything okay?"

"Hello? Theresa?" April's voice crackled

faintly through the radio behind her. "I've got my grandpa. He wants to talk to you. It's important…"

"Hang on." Theresa turned toward the radio. "I've got to take this."

"I told you not to move!" Mandy's voice rose until it cracked. An odd metallic click sounded behind Theresa. She turned.

There was a small handgun in Mandy's gloved hand.

Fear ran cold like water down Theresa's spine.

"Hello?" April's voice grew louder. "Theresa? Can you hear me? Hello? Grandpa, I don't know where she is. Maybe she's on another channel."

"Mandy, please!" Theresa pleaded. "Let me talk to her. They want to help us."

The radio went to fuzz. Her heart sank.

Mandy stepped across the room, holding the gun out in front of her with one hand like she was trying to keep it as far away from her own body as possible. Instinctively Theresa backed up across the room. Her hands rose.

"Tell me what's going on, Mandy. You don't need that gun. I'm here for you and I want to help."

"I need to get out of here," Mandy said. "Now. Do you have a car?"

"I'm sorry, I don't. But Alex has a truck at his cottage, and we can all go get it together when the snow stops."

"I need to get out of here, now!" Mandy's voice rose to a yell. "I need to get to Tanner! Or else somebody's going to kill him!"

The cottage door flew back so hard it clattered.

"Mandy!" Alex's voice sounded so firm and strong it seemed to reverberate against the walls. "Drop the gun. Now."

He stepped through the door, followed by Zoe. Relief and confusion jostled with fear inside Theresa's mind.

Mandy spun toward the doorway. She pointed the gun at Alex.

"Don't come any closer. Please." Mandy's voice quivered. "I don't want any trouble. I just need to get out of here. I need to warn Tanner that you said somebody's trying to kill him."

Alex glanced at Zoe for a fraction of a second. Then, without a word being spoken between them, Zoe slowly slipped sideways, circling around the corner of the room. Instinctively Mandy stepped back toward Theresa.

"Theresa, stay back against the wall and don't move unless I tell you to." Alex's voice was sharp enough to cut glass. "Mandy, look at me. You don't have to worry about any of that. Trust me, it's not your concern. Zoe and I are responsible for your safety, and will make sure the correct people are notified about Tanner and everything else that's happened up here this weekend. But for now, we're all stranded here in the snow until morning. So here's what's going to happen. You're going to drop the gun, right now, and stop this silliness. Because I don't want to hurt you. But I will if I have to."

What was Alex thinking? She'd told him how emotionally fragile Mandy was. She'd warned him that the very last thing Mandy needed was to be talked down to and treated like a child. Clearly he hadn't listened. Mandy took another step back until she was only a few feet away from her. Theresa took a small step forward. Mandy was so close. Just an arm's length away.

"Theresa." A warning rumbled through Alex's voice like thunder, as if reading her mind. "I told you to stay back and let me handle this."

Mandy's eyes darted from Alex ahead of her to Zoe slowly coming around on her left.

"I'll shoot you! Don't you get that?" Mandy's limbs shook harder. Her voice rose so high it broke. "You all act like I don't know what's really going on. But I do. I need to leave, right now. And if you don't let me go, I'll pull this trigger"

"Mandy!" Alex said. "Look at me. You're not going to pull the trigger. You are going to put that gun down. I'm going to count to three and then you're going to drop it. Got it? One—"

Mandy raised the gun. Her eyes closed.

"Two—"

She pulled the trigger.

TWELVE

Something popped. Theresa leaped, grabbing Mandy from behind and knocking her to the floor. They fell together on the carpet. For a moment Theresa was caught in a tangle of limbs, as Mandy thrashed and fought to get free. There was another pop, this one right beside her ear. Then she saw Zoe yank Mandy back and wrestle the gun from her hands. Mandy scrambled to her feet and dashed out into the snow. Alex groaned.

"I'll go after Mandy." Zoe dropped the gun on the table. "You stay with Theresa."

"Thanks," Alex said. Zoe disappeared out into the snow. Alex stretched his hand down toward Theresa. "Well, I guess that could've gone worse."

She grimaced. Was he intentionally trying to remind her of what she'd said to him when they'd gone rolling over the hill? If so, she didn't appreciate it. She grabbed his hand just long enough to let him pull her up, but let go the moment she was on her feet.

"What happened?" she asked. "Where did Zoe and Mandy even come from? How did Mandy get a gun?"

"They were hiding in a bunkhouse in the woods." Alex picked up the gun from where Zoe had left it and opened the chamber. Four pellets dropped out into his hand. "The gun was toy, albeit a pretty realistic one. Had me fooled until she tried to pull the trigger. I was briefing Zoe on the main floor and Mandy must've overheard some of what we were saying, overreacted and snuck out the second story window. This whole thing's ridiculous. The last thing we needed was a runaway client on top of everything else." He tossed the pellets into a metal bucket by the fireplace. "You should never have tackled her. You should've listened to me."

"Excuse me!" Her arms crossed. Why was he talking to her like a naughty child who'd stayed out past her curfew? "I was right behind her. You had Zoe circling around to tackle her, right?"

"Yes, but—"

"But I was right behind her!" Theresa said.

"I was already in position. Plus, I'm her psychotherapist. She was clearly upset about something and you clearly were totally dismissing her. You could've used me to help calm the situation down instead of barking at me to stay put."

Alex's eyes rose to the ceiling. He dropped down on the couch. "With all due respect, I don't want you tackling somebody who's armed. You don't know what you're doing!"

"And you do?" Even as the words crossed Theresa's lips she could hear a voice inside her mind telling her to stop. But fear had sent adrenaline pounding through her veins and it was like she couldn't stop. His eyes opened wide. His lips parted. She didn't let him get a word in. She'd yielded to Alex too many times. She'd told him far too many times that she wasn't going to argue. This time he was going to listen.

"You let your client slip out a bedroom window! April came back on the line with her grandpa and we lost the opportunity to talk to her because Mandy was waving that replica gun around. Which I thought was real, too, by the way. You want to blame this disaster on me? You left me alone in here, worried and afraid while you had a private little chat with Zoe for twenty minutes! You could've come back, included me in the discussion. You could've let me know what was going on. But, of course, you didn't. Because you never stop and think that what I feel or what I'm going through matters."

The cottage door flew open. Mandy walked in, propelled by Zoe who had a firm grip on her arm. Grimly, Zoe closed the door behind them. Mandy bolted into Theresa's old bedroom and slammed the door behind her. Seconds later, the sound of hysterical sobbing filtered through the door.

"She doesn't have any weapons on her," Zoe said. "Or anything she could even use as a weapon. I patted her down. She's even more hysterical now than she was this morning."

Zoe glanced for a long moment between Alex and Theresa, her gaze flitting back and forth between the two of them, before finally coming to rest on Theresa. "Am I right in remembering she can't get out that particular window?"

"I think so," Theresa said, nodding. "It's individual stained glass panels and, last I checked, only opens partway. She won't get out without breaking it, which would take a lot of work. She can't sneak out again without us hearing something."

The sobbing rose and fell, mingled with the sound of Mandy cursing.

"Well, it doesn't sound like she's going anywhere now," Zoe said. "She was like a lost deer out there a moment ago. Couldn't figure out where to go. The snow's really coming down. Can't see more than a foot in front of your face. But I think we should make sure someone is awake and on her door all night." Zoe gave Alex a long, firm look that said volumes Theresa couldn't read. "I'm going to go double-check the window from the outside, just in case, and also do a quick perimeter sweep while I'm at it. I trust the two of you have it handled in here."

Zoe slipped out into the snow, leaving them alone again, without waiting for an answer.

"Mandy's really worried about Tanner," Theresa said. "She says she knows something about what's going on up here. I want to go in there and talk to her."

Alex's arms crossed. "You're kidding me. She just threatened your life."

"I deal with upset people for a living. She's hardly the first person to threaten my life, and definitely not the most dangerous!"

"I'm sorry, but no." Alex sat down on the couch. "I don't want you to get hurt."

"Do you think I like the idea of you getting hurt any better?" Theresa dropped down beside him, suddenly feeling like the last drops of adrenaline had been drained from her body. "How many times have you been hurt since I've met you? How many broken bones, stitches and sprains did I nurse you through? But I never once asked you not to jump off some cliff or stop speeding around the rocks. Because I knew you could handle it. Just like I'm positive you'll be an excellent part of Ash Private Security, if you decide to stick it out. Which I hope you do, because it suits you."

There was a long pause. Then Alex chuckled. His hand waved toward the closed bedroom door. "Well, I'm not quitting after my first major failure, now am I?"

She smiled. She liked this side of him. The kind that faced defeat with good humor and kept trying. His gaze drifted up to the ceiling. A silent prayer crossed his lips.

"Okay," he said. "You go talk to Mandy. I can't deny you're really good at talking to people and even better at listening. But the door stays open, and I'm listening in. If she threatens you again, I'm putting a stop to it. Deal?"

"Deal." Her shoulder bumped lightly against his. His eyes met hers. And for a moment the space between them seemed to shrink again. Then they stood up and walked over toward the bedroom door. Theresa knocked on it gently. "Mandy?"

There was a pause. Then Mandy said, "What do you want?"

"Can you open the door?" Theresa asked. "I'd like to come in. We need to talk about Tanner and I want to ask you if you know anything about a missing trunk."

There was another pause that seemed way too long for Alex's liking. Then there was a click and Mandy opened the door. Theresa stepped into the room. Mandy was curled up on a weird, love seat–type thing in the corner of the room. Theresa sat beside her. Not touching her. Not saying anything. Just sitting there. Alex stood on the threshold, not knowing what to do or what to say. He was a big fan of taking action and doing things. She hadn't been wrong when she'd said that back when they'd dated she'd been the brains and he'd been the brawn. Now, faced with someone who'd just threatened her life, and who

Theresa thought could know something important, Theresa was just sitting, doing absolutely nothing.

He closed his eyes for a moment, feeling the silence of the moment pressing around him. He prayed for patience and guidance. Then he found himself praying that God would guide Theresa and help her know what to do.

And that God would show him how to work with her.

Mandy sniffled a little. The sound reminded him of a kitten. When he opened his eyes again, she looked even younger than twenty, sitting in the darkness beside Theresa.

"Can I give you a hug?" Theresa asked.

"Okay." Mandy nodded. The women embraced and then sat back again. Alex crossed his arms and leaned against the doorframe. The clock ticked. Five minutes passed. Then ten. How many times had Theresa sat in silence and listened to him talk, he wondered. She'd always been a good listener—a great listener—in a way that, if he was honest, he'd never been.

"Tanner didn't do anything wrong," Mandy said, eventually. "I heard Alex talking in the bunkhouse, saying how people were getting killed, and cottages were being destroyed, and how Alex thought Tanner was part of it. Well, he's not. I know he's not."

"I didn't know that you knew him all that well," Theresa said. "He's about six years older than you, right?"

"Five and a half," Mandy said. "Almost."

"Did you know he'd been in a car accident?"

Mandy nodded. "I went to see him in hospital this week. He looked so terrible. I couldn't…I couldn't handle it. I started crying and ran out."

"Sounds like it was really hard."

"It was."

Okay, but what did that have to do with anything? Tanner's car accident happened in the city, over a week ago. The two women went back to sitting quietly. Alex's jaw clenched with the effort to keep from talking. Everything inside him wanted to jump in and take charge of the conversation to save himself from having to just stand there, waiting. It was so uncomfortable, he almost laughed at himself.

Okay, Lord, I'm clearly terrible at this. Help me be more like Theresa.

"None of this is Tanner's fault," Mandy said again. "You have to understand that. Tanner's had a really rough life. His dad used to hit him and his mom. Then his dad went to jail. But his mom kept forgiving him and taking him back. So he moved in with his grandparents. That's why he came up to the lake in the summers to stay with them. He had some learning problems at school, which made reading hard, even though he's really smart. The only thing he's really good at is motorcycle racing. But that takes money. Like, lots of money."

Theresa nodded. "Sounds like you care about him a lot."

"I'm in love with him." Mandy's voice grew quiet. "We're dating. Mom and Dad and Emmett and Kyle don't know. Because they all think he's too old for me and not a good person. Because he didn't go to school or get a good job. But he'd never hurt me. He protects me.

"Last summer, this really big jerk was harassing me in town and I was really scared. Tanner saw it was happening, and hauled the guy away, hit him and told him to leave me alone. But then Emmett saw us kissing once and told Mom and Dad, and they all told me I wasn't allowed to ever see Tanner again. Because they wanted me to focus on school, get good grades and be perfect. They thought he'd get in the way of that. But he protected me, you know? He took care of me. You know how special that is?"

"Yeah," Theresa said softly. Her eyes drifted toward where Alex stood in the doorway. "I know how special that is."

Tears coursed down Mandy's cheeks.

Alex had always known that Theresa had been working with Victim Services. But he'd never imagined what it meant to spend all that time just listening to hurting people tell their stories. How could Theresa listen to stuff like this, day after day without having her heart break? He didn't know. He wasn't sure he wanted to. Sure his body could take a lot of hits. But his heart was big and soft. It had wasn't as strong as hers. It never had been.

He turned away. Fumbling in the living room, he found a box of Kleenex on the table. Then he went back to the doorway and stepped into the room sideways, feeling like an interloper.

Theresa took it from his hand and whispered, "Thank you."

"Tanner isn't Castor's friend!" Mandy's voice rose. "Castor is just some guy Tanner knows. I don't know what his real name is, but I know Tanner hates him. Castor texts and orders Tanner to do things, like run out in the middle of the night to sell drugs or buy drugs. Always criminal stuff Castor doesn't want to do for himself. I get worried. But Tanner says that Castor has something on him. Something major. Castor is blackmailing him, and that if he doesn't do what Castor wants something bad could happen. Really bad."

She looked down at her hands and crumpled the Kleenex into a tiny ball.

"Three weeks ago, Tanner heard there was this box of stuff somebody had up at the cottage. Important stuff."

"Who told him about it?"

"Corey Patterson." Mandy's eyes were locked on her hands. "Tanner told me that if he could find it then Castor would leave him alone, forever. So we came up here one weekend and tried to break into a few cottages looking for it. But we didn't find it. And we didn't steal anything. Then he had an accident and ended up in the hospital—" Another bout of sobs overtook her body. Her thin form shook. "I came up here this weekend to try to find it on my own. But, look, I don't know what kind of treasure it is, or where it's hidden. And he never told me who Castor was, or why he was blackmailing him, or any of that. Because he's always protected me. Always. He's stupid sometimes, and he does stupid things. But he's got a good heart and he's always protected me."

Her words dissolved into sobs again. Alex felt a hand brush his elbow from behind. He turned around. Zoe was standing behind him. He'd been so absorbed in listening, he hadn't even noticed her come in. He followed her back into the living room.

"You catch any of that?" he asked, softly.

"Enough." Zoe nodded. "I can't even say I'm surprised. If Tanner was involved in illegal activity, Castor could be any number of criminals or drug dealers he's crossed, or even someone his dad knew."

"Corey Patterson's not looking too great right now, either," he said. They walked over to the couch. The radio was still hissing quietly. April hadn't returned. He switched it off to save the battery and prayed that April's grandfather had believed her and taken action.

"Mandy won't make it out that window, not without breaking it to pieces," Zoe said. "So, as long as she stays in that bedroom she's not going anywhere. But I wish we'd known the game she was playing at before we came up here. I was too easy on her, because she's

Josh's second cousin. But the fact their late grandparents were brothers doesn't mean much at the end of the day. Now, I'm tempted to suggest to Daniel we screen all potential clients, whether they're acquaintances or not."

They sat.

"Theresa's really good," he said slowly. "Like, amazingly good. I'd never seen her in action before today or really understood why it mattered so much to you, Daniel and Josh that she consulted for us. But I don't know anyone else who could've gotten Mandy talking the way she did."

"She has a real knack for calming people down and getting them to trust her," Zoe said. "And, thanks to her, we now know how Castor found out about this trunk, and that both Tanner and Corey are connected to it, too. But we still don't know where it is or what's in it. Any idea how long it will take us to get from here to our cottage on foot?"

"On a good clear day I can run it in twenty-eight minutes and thirty-one seconds." The answer shot out of his mouth so automatically, Zoe blinked. "Or, at least, I used to be able to. In knee-deep snow tomorrow, of course, it would probably take closer to an hour, maybe even more, especially if Mandy gives us trouble."

"I'll warn you right now," Zoe said, "she won't walk very fast."

A cold breeze brushed his skin. Winter wind was seeping in through the cracks around the door. He'd have to strengthen the frame before he fell asleep or somebody else could try getting the door open the same way he had. Even with the roaring fire in the hearth, the cottage was growing colder by the moment.

"We should all sleep in here on the main floor," he said, "with our boots on and winter gear at hand, so we're ready to go in case anything happens. You and I can take turns keeping the fire going. I want to keep a close eye on the storm and be prepared to leave here the moment it breaks, even if that means traveling in the dark. I'm counting on the fact that Castor and whatever other thugs there might be left that are conducting this cottage-to-cottage search will lay low until sun up."

There was a creak on the floorboards behind them. He looked over his shoulder. Theresa slipped out of the downstairs bedroom. She closed the door behind her.

"I don't think we're dealing with more than

two thugs at this point," she said. "Three if you count Gnat. The original attack on the cottage involved Castor, Brick and Howler. Brick and Howler are now dead. That leaves just Castor and whoever the other man was who tried to grab me off the snowmobile at the safe house. Honestly, I thought it was Castor at first. He was equally huge and menacing. But I split Castor's lip head butting him. This guy's mouth was fine."

She frowned and sat down on the arm of the couch beside Zoe.

"How's Mandy?" Alex asked.

"Not good," Theresa said. "But she needed some time to be alone with her own thoughts and I'm hoping she'll manage to sleep. She's beyond exhausted and that's making everything harder. But at least now we know why she's been so anxious. I still don't think she's being fully honest with us, but I think that's because she's not being fully honest with herself. She's lying to herself about something. You can see it in her eyes. But I believe she is telling the truth about her feelings for Tanner. She's really deeply into him. Infatuated. Even fixated."

Alex ran both hands through his hair and groaned. "So, we've got actual criminals, using real weapons to destroy people's lives, and the only reason the four of us are caught in the middle of this mess is because some straight-A student from a prominent, success-ful family has an irrational crush on a degen-erate bad boy."

"Just because other people don't understand their relationship doesn't mean it's irrational." Theresa's smile grew thin.

"Doesn't mean it's real love either." Alex's eyes met hers over the top of Zoe's head.

"It's real to her."

Theresa could feel the heat of Alex's gaze locked on her face. But she didn't look away, even as she could see the tension crackling in the depths of his eyes like kindling in a fire.

Zoe stood up. "I'm going to go upstairs and see if I can find some blankets."

She slipped up the stairs. Neither Alex nor Theresa turned to watch her go.

"So you're going to defend Mandy for dat-ing a criminal behind her family's back and lying to us about her real reason for coming up here?" Alex asked.

"No, of course I'm not. But I'm going to try to understand her!" Theresa said. She slid off the arm of the couch into the space Zoe had just left. "Sometimes relationships don't make sense to the people watching from the outside. Based on what she said her parents and brothers thought of her dating Tanner, this definitely seems to be one of those times. But, for whatever reason, Mandy feels like there was something important that was missing from her life. She found that something in Tanner. Sounds like he found that something in her, too. That's what romantic attraction is. Two people finding the missing piece of themselves in each other."

Alex could feel his chest tighten as his heart beat against his rib cage. It was like he was suddenly aware of Theresa's every breath rising and falling, and every freckle on her fire-lit skin. It was like something inside him had been waiting years to be sitting beside this woman, in this room, by this fire, but he'd forgotten what he was supposed to do and say now that he was here.

Then he felt the side of her hand brush his. He took it and looped his fingers through hers. Not knowing what to say. Not knowing what to do, yet holding her hand tightly, like the very first time they'd ever held hands as teenagers and knowing they didn't want to ever let go.

He'd never felt for another woman what

he'd felt for Theresa. Sure, he'd seen other women who were attractive and had wonderful qualities. He'd had well-meaning friends and family members nudge him toward one woman or another.

But Theresa was like a piece of his own heart that had somehow slipped out of his chest and into the world in the shape of a strong, beautiful, talented, compassionate woman. He'd felt safe with her, which was something he'd never felt with anyone. He'd felt braver, believed in and desperate to be a better man for her sake. Despite every other amazing friendship and family relationship he had, nothing in his life compared to that. Nothing ever had.

But what did he have to offer her back? She'd told him the day they'd ended their engagement that she wanted a stable, secure man with a strong foundation beneath him. She deserved that. He was still a work in progress.

He dropped her hand and stood, crossing his arms over his chest before he gave into the temptation to kiss her again.

"Well, I'm sure you also tell your clients that attractions don't always last," he said. "When Zoe and I get her out of this alive, I hope Mandy learns to make better choices.

I'm going to go see if Zoe needs help. The snow should erase any trace of our tracks, but still it would be good for her and I to go over escape routes and access points."

He crossed the floor to the bottom of the stairs. Then he stopped and looked back.

"For the record, you did a great job disarming Gnat," he added. "Your instincts were great. If you are going to consult on more Ash clients, I know a really good self-defense class I can recommend back in the city. Again, your instincts are great and you're clearly strong. I'm sure you'll get a lot out of it."

"Thank you." She hadn't moved from her place on the couch. "I might take you up on that."

A slow smile crossed his face.

"If someone ever tries choking you again, like Brick did, a good elbow to the face works," he said. "And next time you leap for a gun, make sure you've disabled your opponent with a good blow first, so you won't have to risk fighting them for the weapon. Also, when Castor first broke into the cottage, I noticed you went for the saber over the fireplace. Don't discount things like chairs and tables as defensive weapons. Doing something unexpected and being spontaneous helps."

She nodded slowly, and silence fell for a long moment between them.

"You should hold workshops on stuff like this," she said. "You'd be really good at it."

She believed in him. The thought hit him like a sucker punch. Theresa believed in him. She probably had no idea how good that felt to know.

"Thank you." He turned and started up the stairs to the second floor, feeling his feet dragging heavily with every step.

Help me, God. What am I doing? I thought I'd turned my back on my feelings for her. But now I'm feeling like a foolish kid who can't control his own heart. I'm still not the kind of financially stable husband material she was looking for. I've never been what she needed.

Zoe was standing at the top of the stairs, buried in an overflowing armful of blankets.

"I'm going to do another quick sweep of the top floor, too," he said. "See if there's anything we missed."

"Okay." Zoe's eyebrow rose. But she stepped aside. "I'm going to check in on Mandy again and see about setting up some beds downstairs. We should also eat."

"Theresa packed some emergency rations. I'm sure she has enough to feed an army."

He started walking along the upstairs landing. But the sound of his sister's voice made him stop and look back.

"I'm so sorry." Zoe was still standing at the top of the stairs. "These past few months I pushed you too hard to forgive Theresa and reconcile with her. I didn't get it. I thought you were holding back because of stubbornness and a bruised ego. I didn't realize you still had really strong feelings for her."

"Don't worry about it." He raised his chin. "It doesn't matter what I do or don't feel, because I'm not going to act on it. All that matters is that it won't get in the way of all of us getting out of here alive."

THIRTEEN

They left before the sun was up, walking single file in the knee-deep, pale gray snow. Theresa's eyes rose to the faint glimmer of dawn beginning to seep into the edges of the horizon and she stifled a yawn. Even knowing that Alex and Zoe had been sleeping in shifts, she'd barely managed to sleep herself. Breakfast had been quick and tense and no more than a few bites of granola washed down with tea made over the fire. Now her whole body ached with fatigue and a pain that made it feel like her body was nothing but a collection of bones that had forgotten how to work together.

Broken branches and ice-cracked trees filled the forest. Alex led the way, trampling down the snow, while Zoe brought up the rear, keeping Mandy close in front of her. Theresa walked four paces behind Alex, staring at the long, strong lines of his form, a deep blue silhouette in the early morning light. He led them slowly, deliberately, through the trees, keeping away from both the road and the exposed beaches, as he followed the shoreline. The forest cracked around them with breaking limbs and falling ice that sounded in the forest like gunfire. As they rounded one bend, the sound of tires spinning in the snow sent them sprawling low to the ground. More than once, as they reached a cottage or a break in the forest, Alex stopped and silently held up a hand, then gestured for them to crouch and wait while he went on ahead, leaving her with her heart thumping in her chest until he came back and declared the coast clear.

She couldn't help but watch him. It was like she'd spent the past twenty-four hours with an amazing and breathtaking stranger, who now lived inside the body of the man she'd once loved more than anything else in the world. He was so determined, self-assured and confident in the task he was called to do. She'd begged God on bended knee, when they were much younger, for the cute, long-legged, blond jock who'd swept her heart away in a glance to hurry up and grow into a man she could marry. Yet somehow every time she prayed, she'd imagined it would mean him giving up the well-worn blue jeans, quick athletic impulses and great outdoors for some kind of "real job."

Lord, how was I so wrong? How did I think that loving Alex meant pushing him to be something that he was never meant to be?

They reached the final turn of the bay and she saw Cedar Lake spread out ahead of them, like a glittering sheet of diamonds, with Joshua's father's cottage up ahead of them through the trees, and Alex and Zoe's family cottage beyond it, with its beautiful, two-story boathouse sitting high on the water's edge. They kept going, until finally, through a break in the trees, they could see the solid, snow-covered shape of Alex's truck sitting by the cottage's back door.

He paused and turned back. A smile crossed his face and as he raised his eyes to the sky, the bright rays of the rising sun seemed to pool in his eyes. "Okay, team, we're almost there. Our cottage is still standing, none of the windows are broken and it looks like my truck is still there. Once we dig the truck out, we should hopefully be ready to go."

He slipped away from the group and went on ahead again. They were just a few minutes away from the whole ordeal at Cedar Lake being over. Then what? She and Alex would part ways again, and he'd go back to being somebody she just used to know? Last night, by the firelight, with the feel of his kiss still lingering on her lips, she'd been swept up in the pain of not getting the life with Alex that she'd wanted.

But what would've happened if they hadn't ended their engagement? Would Alex have stuck with a career path he'd hated and never found his calling? Would she have ever had a reason to fill her loneliness with volunteering, eventually working with Victim Services, spending countless hours helping people in trouble? Would she even have her own psychotherapy practice? Would they have ended up like so many of the couples who came to her for counseling, wondering how the love they'd once felt had grown dull and the life they'd thought they'd wanted turned sour?

If she'd met him now, without their history, she wouldn't care that he lived with his sister or had recently helped start a new company. That anxious young woman she'd been was long gone. She was stronger now, braver and less fearful of the future. She had her own business, her own home, and had seen how her parents weathered their financial storm together.

She was finally ready to find a partner to weather the storms with, instead of looking for somebody to save her. But would Alex ever want to risk a future with her, considering how very badly they'd hurt each other? They were so different. Too different. But she was thankful that the fear and anxiety she'd felt over her parents' financial calamity hadn't driven them into living a life so much smaller than the one they'd both ended up living. They'd both found a life that had given them joy.

Even if that life hadn't included each other.

Alex darted back and slipped into the trees beside them.

"It looks good," he said. "Roads are terrible, but despite the weather forecast, it's nothing a four-wheel drive with good snow tires can't handle. There's no disturbed snow around the truck. There's no evidence the cottage was broken into. My laptop is exactly where I'd left it. The power is out, though, and the phone is down. Thankfully, we're not planning on staying long."

Relief spread through Theresa's limbs. *Thank You, God!* It was almost over. Just a few moments to clear off the truck, then they'd be able to drive away from Cedar Lake.

Alex blew out a long breath. He glanced toward the boathouse down by the frozen water. "I've got to run a quick errand before we go. There's something I left in the boathouse a long time ago that I should probably go get. You okay getting a start on clearing off the truck?"

Zoe's eyes searched her big brother's face with a look Theresa couldn't decipher. "You sure?"

He nodded. "Yeah. It's time."

What was this all about?

Zoe pressed her lips together. Then she nodded quickly. "Okay. I'd come help you, but I should stick with Mandy and Theresa. Just hurry back, okay?"

"Don't worry. I'll be back before you're even done clearing off the truck."

Theresa's eyes rose to the horizon. The sun was rising over the treeline, sending long shadows spreading over the snow. What was Alex chasing after now? What could possibly be so important that he'd risk delaying them?

She took a deep breath.

Lord, please help me trust that Alex knows what he's doing.

* * *

For a moment, Alex paused. Theresa's deep green eyes were on his face, with a look that seemed to peer straight through to his core, making him wish for a moment that he could reach up into the sky and rip away the last eight and a half years like pages of a book that should never have been written. Then he pushed that thought away. No, he didn't regret the man he'd become, the path he'd trod or the vocation he'd found. Not for an instant. He'd just wished it had all included her.

I failed you, Theresa. But I've got another chance and I'm going to try to make it right.

"Don't worry," he said again. "I'll be back before you know it."

He turned and moved as quickly as he could through the deep snow toward the boathouse. Last night, he'd lain awake on the cottage floor by the fire, watching the wood turn to ash, while his mind had burned with regret. How had he failed her so badly? Why hadn't be fought for her? Why did he just demand the engagement ring back, only to storm into the upper room of the boathouse and throw it so hard it had fallen through the floorboards?

A ring he hadn't been able to afford. But he'd wanted it, selfishly and arrogantly, because he'd been so fixated on giving her the very best. So, he'd gotten his first credit card and maxed it out just to be able to buy it. Shame burned in Alex's heart as he remembered how the man he'd thought would be his father-in-law had warned him off the dangers of debt and gave him the cash to pay off the card.

Had Theresa's father known that day how close to financial ruin he was then? Maybe. But Alex knew well enough what had happened to that ring a year later. As a surprise to his bride-to-be, Alex's father and Josh had helped him transform the upper floor of the boathouse into a small, one-bedroom apartment so that he and Theresa could have their own special living space on the lake. When the engagement was broken, Alex had felt like trashing the whole place. Instead, he'd just stormed in there and thrown the ring as hard as he could.

What an idiot he'd been.

If he'd let her keep it, she could've sold it to help pay her parents' mounting bills or reimburse the deposits her parents had lost on the canceled wedding. Or, if they'd refused to accept the money from her, the woman he'd loved could've still used it to buy a car or help pay for university or put a down payment on a place to live. Anything. Instead, he'd just tossed away the most valuable thing either of them had ever owned.

He wasn't that man anymore. He might not be able to make up for the mistakes he'd made. But he could take a five-minute detour to fish the ring out of the floorboards, to help put things right now and make sure one good thing came from his trip to Cedar Lake.

His long strides took him down to the lake, breaking the fresh, unmarked snow. Something like hope lifted his heart. He reached the boathouse. The large sliding front door was still open from when he'd flown out on the snowmobile to save Theresa. But blowing snow had wiped the snowmobile tracks clean. He slipped into the boathouse and up the narrow wooden stairs to the second-floor apartment.

The door was ajar. He slipped inside. Boxes of neglected possessions that he hadn't been around to use packed the room. He wove his way through the equipment over to the window, passing water skis, rappel gear, sports equipment, and household items he'd gathered to set up their apartment with. There were even boxes of his old clothes that he'd left unopened and neglected for years. He'd forgotten all this was here. It was as if his memories of Cedar Lake had been buried under a thin sheet of ice that he'd been skimming over for years, never stopping to look at what lay below in case the ice broke and he went tumbling through. How patient his parents and sister must've been with him. He owed them an apology, too.

Lord, I'm sorry I didn't deal with all this sooner. Thank You for helping me realize I had to step up and face my past with Theresa. Thank You for helping me see that I needed to truly forgive her. Thank You for helping me see it was time to stop hiding and running from the mistakes I'd made, too, instead of putting all the blame on her.

He reached the corner of the room and dropped to his knees. His eyes scanned the dark and dusty floorboards. For a long, agonizing moment he didn't see anything. Then he saw it. A glint of light was shining in the darkness. Carefully, he pried the glittering gold-and-diamond band from between the floorboards. His fingers closed over it. He started to stand slowly, carefully sliding the found treasure into his pocket.

He heard the creak of the floorboards behind him too late.

"Stay there," a wavering voice said behind him. "Hands up. Or everybody dies."

It was Gnat.

FOURTEEN

Alex rose to his full height and turned. Gnat's sweatshirt was bloodstained, and even with a hat and scarf obscuring his face Alex could tell Gnat's skin was gray and clammy. A gun was clenched in Gnat's hand. Alex felt his limbs tense to strike. The space was tight and cluttered. Would Gnat even get a shot off? But even as the thought crossed his mind, he remembered how Theresa had talked Mandy down, and what she'd said about Gnat. *"Find out what he knows. He's frightened, panicked and desperate. But I think he'd only kill if he was cornered and had no choice."*

"Okay, I hear you." Alex's hands rose. "I don't want to hurt you. I'm pretty sure you don't want to hurt me. You need help. Why don't you put down that gun and come with my friends and me in my truck? And I'll make sure you get to a hospital."

"I'm not going anywhere without the trunk." Gnat's eyes darted to the window. The light fell on his face. And for the first time, Alex got a good look at the frightened eyes behind the scarf.

"It's you, Tanner, isn't it?" Alex stepped closer, as a huge part of the puzzle he'd been chasing through the snow suddenly began to make sense. "You came up here to find the trunk for Mandy, because Castor's blackmailing you. That's what you meant when you told Theresa that Castor had run you off the road. You were referring to the accident in the city that put you in the hospital. That's why you're bleeding. You burst your stitches coming up here."

Tanner looked down at the floor and Alex knew that he had him dead to rights. "How do you know all that?"

"Because a really good friend of mine is really good at listening to people," Alex said. *And she can make me better at being the man I'm supposed to be.* He risked taking a step closer. "What's in the trunk, Tanner?"

"Proof that Castor is a criminal. So I can't leave until I've got it. Otherwise he'll find it and destroy it, and then he'll keep making me

do things I don't want to do, just so I can protect Mandy. You get that, right?"

*I get that you believe it's true, and Theresa
said that's what matters.*

"Where's Zoe's car?" he asked. "How did
you get here without leaving footprints?"

"I tried to drive it across the lake but it
crashed through the ice." He shifted his feet.
"I barely made it out before it sank. I came
over the ice so I wouldn't leave footprints. I
knew you had a truck, but I was going to sleep
a bit and wait until the snow stopped before
I took it. I didn't want to drive when it was
coming down that bad."

Alex nodded. "So, what's your move here,
Tanner? How are you going to find the trunk
and get it out of Cedar Lake with nobody
stopping you? Do you even know where it is?"

Tanner shook his head. "No, but I've got
someone who does. He has to. And I'm going
to make him tell me."

The young man with the gun moved backward and gestured Alex toward the doorway
of what would've been the bedroom.

Oh, no.

Emmett Rhodes, the car salesman, Mandy's
big brother and Josh's second cousin, now
sat tied on the floor in the dingy, dark room.

The large man's hands were bound behind his back. A crude piece of duct tape covered his mouth. Anger burned in Emmett's eyes. A sleeping bag and junk food wrappers lay on the old camp bed in the corner. Emmett must've come up, as threatened, to collect Mandy himself and somehow decided to come into the boathouse where Tanner had gotten the better of him.

Lord, please help me know what to do.

"Let me talk to him," Alex said. "Let me ask him if knows anything about the trunk."

"He'll lie to you!" Tanner's voice rose. "Don't you get it? He's trying to find it, too. You can't let him have it! Or he'll stop me from being with his sister. You can't make me do something that means I can't ever see Mandy again."

Emmett's eyes met Alex's, dark with rage. An arrogant, powerful, litigious man whose family hired them to watch his sister now lay bound at his feet. Emmett shook his head forcefully. No, he seemed to be saying, no he didn't know anything about the trunk. The only reason Alex had to not fight Tanner and free Emmett was the word of a petty criminal.

Lord, I need Theresa here now. Please, help me to think like her and see what she'd see.

Theresa didn't think Tanner was a killer, and it was worth trying to talk him down. Theresa thought the love Tanner and Mandy shared was real. But was Alex really willing to risk everything he'd built on her snap assessment of someone who'd clearly kidnapped a man and was now holding a gun on them?

"I don't know everything that's going on." Alex took a deep breath. He could see Tanner shaking. "But I do know one thing for certain. Theresa tells me that Mandy loves you, Tanner. Mandy loves you, like, a whole lot. And she doesn't want you to spend the rest of your life in jail for hurting her brother and me. She's waiting right outside by my truck. She wants to see you. But I can't let you go out there and see her as long as you're waving a gun and holding people hostage. Love means protecting people—you told her that. Sometimes that even means protecting them from the worst parts of ourselves."

For a long moment he prayed silently as Tanner stood there, frozen, with the gun in his hands, like he couldn't decide whether to shoot or run. Then he yanked his scarf off and Alex looked into the face of the guy he'd met on the lake so many years ago.

"I never killed anybody," Tanner said. "I

promise. I did some bad stuff. I sold and bought drugs for Castor. But not that. I never hurt anybody. I wouldn't. You got that, right?"

What on earth could he say to that? What would Theresa say?

"I hear you," Alex said again. "Now, I'm going to count to three and you're going to drop the gun. Once that's done I'm going to let Emmett go, and we're going to take you to the hospital, okay?"

"Am I going to jail?" Tanner asked.

"Probably." Alex took another step forward. "But being jailed is much better than dead. Second chances are worth risking a lot for, especially when you've got somebody who cares about you. Now, you're going to drop the gun for me. On three. One—"

Tanner hesitated.

"Two—" Alex stepped to the side and, in one smooth movement, twisted the gun from Tanner's hand and simultaneously dropped the young man to the floor.

"Three," Alex said softly. Firmly but gently, he pulled Tanner's hands behind his back and tied them together with a piece of boat rope. The look of regret in Tanner's eyes was so deep, Alex's heart ached. *Lord, have mercy on this foolish man. Help him find his way.*

Alex set him down carefully on the bunk in the corner. Then he walked over and swiftly pulled off Emmett's gag.

"You're fired," Emmett snapped, "I'm suing you and destroying your life, your family and your private security company."

There wasn't a mark on the man's face or any obvious bruises on his body. However Tanner had gotten the better of him, he clearly hadn't struck him hard, let alone gotten up the courage to hurt him. Alex stepped around behind him and released Emmett's hands. They were huge.

"I'm sorry you feel that way—"

"You're sorry I feel that way!" Emmett's voice rose to a bellow. Anger tore like fire through his voice. Emmett stretched his long arms out and cracked his knuckles. "You took my baby sister up here without doing me the courtesy of telling me that my parents had hired you. You let some creep kidnap me and then stood around listening to him rant while I was tied up. I knew the moment I saw your name attached to Ash Private Security that it was a total joke."

"Again, I'm sorry," Alex said. His jaw clenched but he didn't give Emmett the satisfaction of letting even one inch of his frustration sound in his voice. "I took your sister over to your family cottage on the other side of the lake. There was some trouble, but we're all together now and can all head back to the city. Now, where did you park your car? I've only got the one truck and there's not enough space for all of us."

"My car is none of your concern." Emmett's huge bulk filled the doorway. "Here's what's going to happen. I'm going to take Mandy and that creepy little insect in the corner back to the city in your truck and make sure he gets dropped off at the police station. Then I'll send somebody back here to pick up you, your sister and your finicky little princess."

Finicky little princess. The words Alex had dismissed as meaningless, the words he'd spat out to his friends in anger the day the engagement had been broken, were now coming from Mandy's brother's mouth. Alex felt his smile go tight. He grabbed Tanner by the shoulder and steered him past Emmett to the stairs, praying hard with every step.

"Theresa's a pretty amazing person," Alex said. "She's the absolute best. I'm very thankful to her for helping me see things I needed to see."

Out of the corner of his eye he saw Emmett's arm swing high. Alex let go of Tanner and swung back. But it was too late. Emmett was pointing a gun at him. A sneer turned on his lips. "You really shouldn't have stumbled into this, Alex. You're not cut out for playing with the big boys. You never were."

Alex's hands rose. "You're Castor?"

But how? And why? How would he ever warn Zoe and Theresa?

Then, to his surprise, he saw Tanner shake his head.

"No, not quite," Emmett snarled. "But I'm going to make sure he gets all the blame for killing you two."

Theresa stood beside the truck, her feet in the snow and her gaze tracing Alex's footprints leading down to the boathouse. Alex had been gone too long. The truck was mostly clear. The engine was warming up. She should go after him.

"What are you thinking about?" Zoe's voice snapped her attention back to the truck.

"Nothing. Just wondering what Alex is doing." Theresa flipped the snow brush around and used the scraper side to get the last of the ice off the driver's-side window. The truck's engine purred softly beside her.

Mandy was curled up in the backseat, in a ball, claiming she was too tired to help. It was probably just as well. Mandy had dragged her feet all the way back to the cottage. Youthful angst could be exhausting. "I'm just thankful the truck is running and we should be able to get out of here soon."

"Alex is a good driver and it's a big truck with four-wheel drive. We should be okay," Zoe agreed. "But are you okay? Things between you and Alex seemed a bit intense last night."

Theresa shrugged. Were they intense? Probably. There'd always been some kind of spark between them. It was what to do with that spark that was the problem.

"I got the feeling there was a lot you two hadn't said to each other that needed to be said." Zoe hopped up onto the running board and stretched her long brush over the top of the truck. "You'd be the first person to tell me that living with unresolved things is hard."

Theresa bristled. "I wouldn't say we'd left a lot unresolved."

Zoe gave her a pointed look over the top of the truck. "You never told him the full extent of your parents' financial trouble."

"I tried to tell him. He just didn't listen!"

But the old, automatic, familiar reply sounded hollow and tinny to her ears. She'd been telling herself that same version of the story for so many years. It had become her truth. Yet, was that how it had really happened, all those years ago? Maybe not. "To be honest, I don't know what I told him. I remember it very differently than he does. It was a long time ago. I know I told him that my parents couldn't pay for the wedding and that he needed to get a job and start taking life seriously. But I don't know how much of the blame for what happened is mine and how much is his. We were just a bad match. We were way too different. It never would've worked out. Everybody knew it, probably, and we were the last to know."

"Are you kidding me?" Zoe snorted. "Nobody thought you were bad together or a mismatched couple. I might've only been a teenager back then, but even I knew how disappointed our parents were. Everyone on the lake felt gutted for you guys. The only real criticism I ever heard was that you guys were too young and not ready."

She dropped her brush in the snow and hopped down.

"Okay," Zoe said, "I'm going to tell you

something I thought you already knew, but now I'm guessing you don't. You remember your old wooden hope chest? Well, Josh and his father saved it from the bankruptcy auction. They bought it back for you two. It sat in his cottage living room for days, and people filled it with notes of encouragement and money to help you get started. People even went and returned their wedding gifts and showed up with envelopes of cash to give you guys a fresh start. For whenever you were ready. But you were both so angry, Josh wanted to wait to tell you until you calmed down. Then, of course, he got deployed. But your wedding chest sat there, forever. Because Alex's best friend refused to get rid of it. Because even he thought that whatever you were going through was temporary and you would want it back one day."

Tears rushed to Theresa's eyes. "I always thought it disappeared to some stranger."

"I wanted to tell you." Zoe shook her head. "I don't know why Josh didn't say anything. He's the kind of guy who likes to hold things in and has never been much of a talker. He's a reserved military guy, through and through. My guess is that he didn't want to put pressure on either of you. My mom told me to stay out of it. So I held my tongue. Because what do I know about romance? I've never met anyone I clicked with like you did with my brother. Besides, I was furious at you for way too long. But don't go around saying that nobody believed you two were a good fit. Everybody thought you were perfect for each other. I guess it doesn't matter who believes in your love, if you're not convinced and don't believe in it yourselves."

A gunshot split the air. The glass in the boathouse's upper window shattered.

"Alex!" Theresa dropped the scraper. She tore through the snow toward the boathouse. Fear pounded hard in her heart. Alex was in trouble. She needed to help him.

"Theresa! Stop!" Zoe shouted.

She didn't turn.

Lord, please help Alex. Save him. I don't want to imagine this world without him—

"Theresa, please!" Zoe caught her around the middle and nearly brought her down to her knees. Theresa spun toward her, adrenaline pumping so hard through her veins she almost tried to toss her off. Zoe held her firm. "Stop."

"But Alex is in danger!" A sob of fear choked her voice in her throat.

"I know," Zoe said, and Theresa could see

the fear filling her eyes. "And I'm going to help him. But Alex wouldn't want you in danger, too. Please, go back to the truck. Keep Mandy safe. Do your job. Let Alex and I do ours."

Tears filled Theresa's eyes. Was this how Alex had felt when he'd charged across the unsafe ice to save her? Was this how he'd felt when she'd fallen through the ice and when she'd fought for the gun?

"Keep him safe, please. Don't let him get hurt. Don't let him die."

"I'll do everything in my power to make sure that won't happen," Zoe said. "I promise."

Another gun blast shook the air. Zoe dashed across the snow toward the boathouse. Theresa felt her legs go weak and wobbly beneath her. She sank down into the snow on her knees.

Lord, please, keep them safe. Forgive me for being so hard on Alex and blaming him for mistakes we both made. Please give me the opportunity to tell him.

Then she stood. She might not be a bodyguard, but she was a psychotherapist and a good one. Mandy needed her. She turned back.

The truck door was open. Mandy was gone.

"Mandy!" Theresa screamed. Mandy's footprints disappeared into the woods. Theresa followed. She saw Mandy's back and the flash of blond hair as the teenager disappeared through the trees. "Mandy! Come back!"

What do I do?

Theresa ran after her.

FIFTEEN

Alex wrestled Emmett for the gun. The larger man had managed to get off two shots. Alex had rolled beneath the first as the window shattered above him. Then he had caught Emmett by the knees just as the second bullet hit the wall.

Alex wasn't going to let him get off a third.

Tanner had taken off, racing down the stairs with his hands still tied behind his back, leaving Alex and Emmett locked in a battle for the gun. Alex's hands were clenched over Emmett's hands. Emmett's hands clutched the gun. Alex had never won any kind of physical challenge against Emmett Rhodes before. But there was no way he was going to lose this one.

With one swift move he kicked the car salesman's legs out from under him. Emmett swore as they tumbled to the ground, Alex on top. But Emmett punched out hard. Pain exploded through Alex's jaw, so fiercely that for a moment he almost let go.

Alex bent Emmett's wrists back, forcing the gun from his hands. Emmett bellowed in pain. In one desperate yank, Alex twisted the gun from his hand. It flew across the room. Alex leveled a blow to Emmett's face and dived after the gun. Emmett leaped on his back. Alex's jaw hit the floor.

Then they heard footsteps on the stairs below.

"Is that your useless little princess?" Emmett's hateful voice hissed in his ear. "I ruined her life, you know. I was so sick of her. The finicky little china doll, who was always so slow, weak and fussy about every little thing. She didn't belong up here. She wasn't one of us. But she got all the best toys because of her parents' work. All those perks she didn't deserve, zipping around the lake on fancy sports equipment like she was better than me. So I took everything that mattered to her. Because I could. Because she didn't deserve it. But she didn't know when to quit. So now, I'm going to kill you in front of her and then I'm going to kill her."

Something snarled inside Alex's heart as

he heard the teasing, dismissive, bullying blather that had been whispered about the woman he'd loved far too many times in his youth, now echoed back in his own ears by a monster. Never again. He hadn't stood by her when he should have. He'd never let her down again. Strength coursed through Alex. He reared back. No creep was ever going to hurt her again. He tossed Emmett off and delivered a decisive blow to his jaw. Emmett crumpled to his knees.

Something clicked. They looked up.

"Hands up. Now!" Zoe was standing in the doorway. The gun Emmett had dropped was held steady in her small hands. Alex stepped back, respecting his sister enough to let her take the shot. But Emmett sneered and swaggered toward her.

"Your kid sister? Seriously, Alex?" An ugly snarling laugh filled his ugly mouth. "You think I'm afraid of a little girl?"

He charged at Zoe. She didn't even flinch. A gunshot sounded. Emmett yelped and fell to the floor, a bullet shot clean through the side of his calf. Alex yanked his hands behind his back and tied them tightly.

"Gag him, too. I don't think we want to hear what he has to say," Zoe said. "I never liked him. He always talked to the girls on the lake like we were all beneath him."

Alex slapped a fresh strip of duct tape over Emmett's mouth. "Did you see Tanner?"

"Yeah, Tanner came running past me at a clip and nearly knocked me off my feet. I don't know where he thought he was going, but I didn't let him get far." She grinned. "He's tied up downstairs by the boathouse door. I didn't want Mandy seeing him."

"Probably wise." Now Mandy would have to handle seeing both her boyfriend and her brother.

Alex walked a gagged Emmett slowly down the stairs holding his hands behind his back, taking it slowly. Tanner looked up at them from his seat on the floor.

"Did you figure out which one of these is Castor?" Zoe asked.

"They say that neither of them are," he said. "But Emmett has an interesting claim about ruining Theresa's life. I look forward to finding out what that's all about. Are you okay watching these two if I go tell Theresa what's going on?"

Zoe nodded. "Absolutely."

He didn't know how they were going to handle this. But it was about time he included

Theresa in making the decisions. He hurried outside and around the corner. The sight hit him like a sucker punch to the gut. The truck door was open. Theresa and Mandy were gone.

He ran back to Zoe. "Where's Theresa? They're both gone."

"I don't know." Zoe's face blanched. "Mandy was in the truck and I told Theresa to stay with her."

His eyes searched the footprints leading into the woods. *Oh, Lord, what should I do?* He and Zoe were a team. He'd spent so much of the day before panicked for her safety. He couldn't just leave her alone with two thugs, even if they were bound.

"Go after her." Zoe's face was calm and firm. "I've got this covered."

Emmett started to snicker. It was an ugly, threatening sound. Zoe took his hands firmly and forced them upward. Emmett winced. The muffled laughter stopped.

"Are you sure?" Alex asked.

A determined grin spread across Zoe's face. "Trust me. They're not going anywhere."

He helped her propel Emmett into the truck, where they left him bound and gagged in the backseat. They left Tanner, more gently bound, in the warmer and more comfortable cottage living room.

Zoe stood in the doorway between the two with her hand on the gun.

"I got this," she said again. "I can keep an eye on two thugs. Go."

Alex ran.

Theresa's hand brushed the doorknob of Josh's family cottage. Mandy's footprints led up to the threshold.

"Mandy?" Theresa called. She pulled the door open slowly and stepped inside. Her heart beat in her chest. The hallway was empty. The kitchen was, too.

"In here," Mandy called.

Theresa followed the sound into a large, tidy living room. Mandy knelt on the floor. Theresa stepped toward her. "I realize you were scared and I don't blame you. But you can't just run off like that. It's not safe."

Mandy looked up at her. Books and knick-knacks lay scattered on the floor around her. There was a tartan tablecloth in her hands.

"I found it," Mandy said again. "I don't know how many times I've been in here and didn't even realize it was here." She set the tablecloth down on the floor. "I've been wondering all this time what was going on and what Tanner was talking about. Now I get it."

Theresa stepped around the table. Sunlight fell over the beautiful carved wooden box at her feet. Her heart leaped. It was her hope chest.

"This was about you all the time," Mandy's hands ran over the wood. "Tanner said you might be the only person who knew about the trunk, which is why I tried to lure you up here. Because it's your box."

Theresa stepped forward slowly as the box came into view. The trunk that people were ransacking cottages and killing over was her old hope chest? No wonder they'd seemed so convinced she'd know something about it.

"I had no idea," Theresa said. "This never even crossed my mind. I guess they didn't know the difference between a chest and a trunk. Plus I haven't thought about this in ages."

Mandy opened it slowly. There, on top of her trousseau, sat a large messenger bag. She reached for it. But Mandy picked it up and opened the clasp. Envelopes, big and small, filled the inside. Zoe had told her that people on the lake had left cards as a message of hope that she and Alex would one day find their way back to each other. But her happiness and unexpected gratitude over that clashed with the knowledge that people had been willing to hurt others, ransack and kill for them.

However much money was in these envelopes, it couldn't be enough to kill for. The words she'd told Alex echoed back in her mind. *People kill for all sorts of reasons—desperation, fear, love, jealousy, hate.* Something dark flickered in Mandy's eyes. Which one was this?

"Let me have those." Theresa stretched her hand out and reached for it. "They're mine and Alex's, not yours."

"No." Mandy shoved the letters back into the messenger bag and stood. She clutched it to her chest. "Tanner told me about this. He told me to come up here and find it. He said it would give us what we needed to start a new life together."

Sympathy lurched inside Theresa. But when she spoke, her voice was firm. "No, Mandy. I'm sorry. If you need help that's something we can sit down and talk about. But those are not yours. And I'm not going to let you steal them."

"Tanner wanted me to have it!" Mandy's voice rose. And too late Theresa saw the kitchen knife in Mandy's hand. "He told me that these would make us free of Castor, forever. I know you and Alex had to break up because of money. If you had the money you could've been together. Just like Tanner and I can be together now."

Theresa's heart ached. She stepped forward, feeling the compassion swelling in her heart overwhelm her fear. "No, Mandy, that isn't true. Money isn't what would've fixed my relationship with Alex. Just like it won't fix your relationship with Tanner now. We weren't ready to get married. We were too young, immature and unable to talk through our deeper problems. Sure, I thought it was about money.

"But the fact I never even knew my hope chest was here just proves it wasn't. I wasn't ready for Alex. I loved him with my whole heart, but I wasn't ready to get married. And I never should've blamed it all on him." She took a step closer. "If what you and Tanner have is real love, then you won't need to steal somebody else's wedding presents or threaten somebody with a knife to have the happily-ever-after you deserve. He wouldn't want you to hurt somebody for him, would he? He wants better for you than that. Just like you want better than that for him."

Mandy's hand shook. The knife dropped to the floor. Tears filled Mandy's eyes. Theresa hugged her closely.

"I'm sorry," Mandy said. "I'm just really, really scared."

"It's okay," Theresa said. Footsteps creaked behind her. A sigh of relief moved through her. Alex and Zoe had found them. "It's going to be okay. I know it's hard and scary now. But it's going to be okay."

She turned. A tall, menacing form in a dark ski jacket filled the doorway. His lip was still split and battered from where Theresa had head butted him in the Rhodeses' cottage. Dark eyes glared at her through a ski mask. A hunting rifle was held steady in his hands.

It was Castor.

"You found the trunk!" He sounded almost surprised. "Excellent. Clearly I should've gotten you to help me from the start. Mandy, bring that bag to me and we'll get going."

Mandy's head shook in fear. Theresa's arm tightened around her.

"I know who you are, Castor, and I know what you've done," Theresa said. "You shot up the Rhodeses' cottage. You killed two men.

Take whatever you want, but you're not taking Mandy."

"Don't be ridiculous," Castor said, chucking. "I haven't killed anybody. That was my stupid brother. He's the one who likes violence. I find the *threat* of terrible, hideous violence is usually enough. Of course she's coming with me."

He pulled off his mask. Theresa gasped.

It was Mandy's brother Kyle.

SIXTEEN

Alex's footsteps slowed as he reached the cottage. Three sets of footprints stopped at the door. He slipped around the side of the cottage and looked in the window. Prayers filled his heart as he saw the scene unfold before him. Theresa stood in front of a wooden chest, her arm around Mandy and her limbs shaking.

A man, the spitting image of the man Zoe was now watching in the back of his truck, stood in the doorway with a gun in his hand. *Kyle Rhodes.* Emmett's brother? The politician? It didn't make sense. Why would either of those two prominent and successful brothers kill for the contents of a wooden box? For now, he didn't need to understand. All that mattered was it appeared one of them now had what he wanted and was going to kill Theresa.

He moved slowly around the cottage to the patio door.

"Mandy!" Kyle snapped. "Come here. Now."

A soft cry escaped from Theresa's lips as Mandy slipped from her grasp and ran to her brother. In one swift motion, Kyle grabbed his sister and pulled her hand to his side, pinning her there. Then he gestured the gun at Theresa.

"Hands up!"

"You've been dealing drugs all this time, haven't you?" Theresa said. "You blackmailed Tanner into running your errands and doing your dirty work, because he loved your sister and thought that was the only way to be with her, right? But then his old friend, Corey Patterson, told him about something in this box that would free him from having to do your bidding. So Tanner came up to find it with Mandy, and you ran him off the road in the city and sent him to hospital."

"That was Emmett." Kyle grimaced. "He'd figured out what Tanner was after and thought if he could get to it first, he could blackmail me."

Alex saw understanding dawn in Theresa's eyes.

"Because you're a respected politician with

a lot to lose," Theresa said. She faced the gunman down with a dignity and grace and courage that took Alex's breath away. "This isn't the first time your brother has blackmailed you, is it? When Mandy came up here again, with us, you panicked. You arrived with your lackeys, kidnapped me and made a big show of ransacking your parents' cottage. But then, when you left, your twin brother showed up and actually shot up the cottage and killed Kenneth Brick. No wonder he didn't search the cottage for me. He didn't know I was there. Then he ran Blake Howler off the road, killing him, too. So you went to Emmett's country house and tried to ambush him there. You just weren't counting on Alex, were you? Here the two of you were fighting for something, and he got right in the way."

Alex crept closer. There was one killer but two hostages. Whatever Alex did, there was a possibility one of them would get hurt. He could only save one. But which one? The client that his company had promised to protect? Or the woman for whom his dented heart was beginning to beat again? *Lord, how do I pick who to save?* He'd been forced to choose between his career path and Theresa once before, and now that decision was being thrown back at him again, on a much bigger scale, with the consequences of life or death.

"Shut up. Now!" Kyle barked. "Don't you get it? If I kill you now everyone will think it was Emmett. Nobody is finding out about this. Ever."

"No," Theresa said. Her eyes flickered to the window for just a fraction of a second. Did she know he was there? Then, all too quickly, her eyes locked back on Kyle. "You need to hear what I have to say. Take the messenger bag, if that's what you came for. Let Mandy and I go. It's not too late for you. Think, Kyle. Whatever it is that's in my wedding chest that caused all this trouble, it's now yours."

"Enough." Kyle's lips turned up in a snarl. "If I'd wanted to listen to a fussy, useless little princess yapping, I'd have taken you, instead of her. You think you're going to trick me into letting you live? Get down on your knees. Now. And not another word."

Theresa knelt. Sunlight fell over her limbs, and in that moment Alex saw suddenly what he'd been blind to for far too long. It wasn't a question of one gunman and two hostages he needed to choose between. Because Theresa wasn't a liability. She wasn't a weakness. She was an asset. His strength. She was his friend and a partner in danger. He could trust her with his life.

He just prayed she trusted him. He grabbed a rock from the snowy ground. Held it high above his head.

"Theresa!" he bellowed. "Drop and roll forward, now!"

The briefest hesitation flickered in her eyes. Then she rolled forward, out of harm's way while Alex tossed the rock through the window. Glass exploded into the room. Alex leaped through.

"Get Mandy out of here!" he called "Now!"

Mandy turned and ran out of the room. Theresa scrambled after her. But Kyle grabbed her by the hair and yanked her back, so hard Theresa screamed in pain.

"Take one more step and I'll kill you both. You hear me?" Kyle snarled. Keeping a tight grip on Theresa's long hair, he leveled Alex in his sights and raised the gun to fire. "I'll shoot you first. Then I'll take care of her."

Alex looked at Theresa. His eyes met hers.

He took a deep breath, and let go of every doubt and fear that had held him back from admitting his feelings. He needed her help to get them out alive. He trusted her.

"Remember our conversation in the cottage?" he asked. "What I told you about the unexpected?"

She nodded.

"Now!" Alex shouted. She spun back, jabbing an elbow hard to Kyle's jaw. He lost his grip on her. The gun shot wildly into the ceiling.

"Theresa!" Alex yelled. "Run!"

She ran for the hallway.

Kyle tried to fire again. The weapon jammed. Alex charged. They fell to the ground and rolled in a fury of jabs and blows. Twice now he'd battled a man this size. Twice now unrelenting fists had tried to pummel him into the floor. But this time he was tired and he was trapped down on the ground, unable to get up to his feet. Then a knife appeared in Kyle's hands and Alex swerved and weaved as the two-edged blade flashed just inches away from his skin. Just one mistake, and he'd be slashed. One mistake and it would all be over.

"Alex! Catch!" Theresa's voice rose above the chaos of the blows and the thundering pain. Instinctively his hand reached out into the air to grab what she threw him, and he felt the hard, smooth shaft of a ski pole land in his grasp.

He swung it around like a sword and

knocked the blade from Kyle's hand. Then he pushed it between himself and Kyle, pressing it up against his throat. With a grunt, Kyle rolled off him. Alex scrambled up, twisted his hands behind him and pinned him to the ground.

"Here," Theresa said. He felt her push a roll of duct tape into his hands.

"Thanks." He taped Kyle's hands and mouth. Then he stood.

Theresa stood there beside him—her cheeks flushed, and her eyes and hair wild—in the shattered broken glass and chaos of the cottage. Alex quickly grabbed her hands. He pulled her into the hallway, away from the criminal and into the safety of his embrace.

His arms slid around her back. He pulled her to him. "You're okay, right? Please tell me you're okay."

A smile brushed her lips and lit up her eyes. "I am."

"Thank You, God!" For a moment, his eyes rose in prayer. Then he tightened his grip on her, brushing his lips over hers, kissing her tenderly and burying his face in her hair. "You were spectacular. You were so brave." He pulled back. His eyes fell on her face. "You are incredible."

I love you. I've always loved you, even when I wouldn't admit it to myself. How am I ever going to be worthy of you?

"Alex! Theresa!" A voice sounded in the doorway. "Are you guys okay?"

Alex pulled back. He turned. He blinked. The tall, dark-haired form of his boss, Daniel Ash, was coming through the snow toward him, flanked by two uniformed police officers and another man in plainclothes.

"Absolutely." A smile crossed his face. "You have no idea how good it is to see you."

His boss smiled. "I have some idea. Zoe filled me in on the two men back at your cottage. Police now have them in custody." He looked past him. "Looks like you also have a third. Can I safely assume that's all the criminals you're planning on rounding up here this weekend?"

"Definitely." Alex chuckled. They stepped back as the officers passed him on their way into the living room. "What are you doing here?"

"I got a call at three in the morning from this young man, saying that you were in danger and that he wasn't sure I should trust the local police up here to give me a straight answer, because they might be in the pocket of a corrupt politician." Daniel stepped back and only then did Alex recognize the man standing beside him. It was Corey Patterson. "He was rather insistent and wouldn't take no for an answer."

Alex blinked. Instinctively, his hand reached out to shake Corey's. "I don't understand."

"My daughter was talking to you on the radio and heard the trouble that was happening up here," Corey said. His voice was gentle but his handshake was firm. "My dad tried to call the police, but he wasn't taken seriously. Maybe because it's a small community and everybody knows I have a record. But we suspect Kyle Rhodes pulled some strings with some dirty cops to look the other way about any calls reporting crime up at this lake. When the local police wouldn't listen to me, either, I called Joshua's father, who, to his credit, agreed to listen. Not every man would take a call from a man he didn't like at two thirty in the morning."

Alex nodded. Nor would he be willing to place such a call.

"But we sorted things out well enough," Corey continued. "He seemed happy I'd gone straight and was raising my daughter. He called some police contacts of his and put the fear into them. He also gave me Daniel's number. We met up and made our way here."

"Please thank your daughter for us," Theresa said. "She's an extraordinary girl."

"Well, I missed a bit of the beginning of her life." Corey looked down at his feet. "She doesn't have a mom, really. But we've had an opportunity to turn things around now. Hopefully, you guys will get to meet her soon."

"I'd like that," Theresa said. Then she glanced at Daniel. "What about Mandy?"

"We caught her running through the woods. She's with Zoe now." He pulled a lumpy brown envelope from his inside jacket pocket and handed it to Theresa. "She had this on her. It's addressed to you."

She took it and opened it slowly. Inside was a plain, unmarked videotape with a sticky note on it. It just said "Sorry, Theresa. Hope this helps."

"I don't understand."

"It was your wedding present from me," Corey said. "It's a security videotape from your parents' business the night of the fire. Emmett and Kyle broke in to steal some stuff and then set the fire to cover their tracks. Only the fire raged out of control. I was already caught up in selling drugs back then. So were they, but they were smarter about it than me and never used. I was supposed to steal the security tape for them and destroy it, only I kept it as insurance." He sighed. "Look, I was a mess back then. I don't even remember a lot. But when I heard your folks lost everything in the fire, I snuck it in as a wedding present, thinking it might help. Nobody was talking to me back then, so I did it anonymously, thinking if you knew it was from me, I'd get in more trouble. I forgot about it for years, until Tanner told me how Emmett was blackmailing him. I figured he'd go to the police with it. I never imagined all this would happen."

"So Emmett and Kyle accidentally destroyed Theresa's family business to get away with theft," Alex said. "And then they were willing to ransack cottages and kill for the tape rather than letting evidence of a decade-old crime come to light."

"My parents might even be able to use this to reopen their fight with the insurance company, by proving it was arson." Theresa looked up at Corey. "Thank you for this."

Corey shrugged. "I'm just really sorry I didn't get my life together fast enough to tell you about this a whole lot sooner."

"It's okay. I forgive you." She gave him a quick hug. "Better late than never."

Theresa sat alone on a bench by the frozen water with the satchel of letters and cards. Behind her, chaos reigned. People in uniform seemed everywhere at once. Alex had been swept away from her and pulled into a conversation. Then she lost him completely to the crowd of uniforms. Through her work with Victim Services she'd been to enough crime scenes to know what happened next: the waiting, the questions, the interviews, the feeling like everyone had suddenly become a very important piece of a very important puzzle, but that it was also incredibly important not to say or do anything until those responsible for the scene decided what you needed to do. So until someone told her where to be, she was going to take a moment to sit quietly, thank God and breathe.

The police had taken the videotape, but they'd seemed content to leave her with her cards. Carefully, she pulled the pile of envelopes out onto her lap and started to read. Her eyes misted with tears.

Dear Theresa and Alex,
If the past forty-eight years of marriage have taught us anything, it's that the path is rarely straight and smooth. But it's worth the struggle.
All our love and prayers,
John and Judith Patterson

Two fifty-dollar bills were attached to the card.

To Alex and Theresa,
Heard the wedding was being postponed. Alex, your mom said it was best to take our gifts back and let you sort out what you were doing. Decided to keep the juicer. Here's forty dollars to buy one of your own, or whatever else you guys are after. Not sure what's going on with you, but hope you're well. Remember, never go to bed angry and always say you're sorry.
Bob and Edith Wright

She kept reading, note after note filled with prayers, best wishes and words of advice about marriage, love, life and trusting

God. Something about them made her ache inside. She'd been so hurt when her family had lost the cottage at Cedar Lake, she'd felt like it was a community she'd been pushed out of. Now she saw just how eager they'd been to love her and Alex, and support them even if they didn't know what was going on.

Dear Theresa and Alex,
This is one of the hardest notes I've ever had to write. As I write this, the sun is shining through the cottage window, sending sparkling light dancing over the lake, and the calendar tells me that to-day's the day two of my favorite people were going to get married. My heart is sad. I can't imagine what you two are going through today. Love is hard and painful sometimes.

Alex: I was sixteen when I met your father, nineteen when I got pregnant with you, and twenty when I lost him. At the time I thought the pain would tear me apart from the inside out, and you, my tiny baby, were my lifeline. It took me years before I met Joe, and even more years before I was ready to admit I'd fallen in love again, and he became your stepfather and brought Zoe into our lives. I'm so thankful for you and so proud of the man you've grown up to be.

Theresa: you are such a beautiful person inside and out, and I'm so glad God brought you into our lives and our family. When Alex told me he was going to ask you to marry him, I wasn't in favor of it at first. You both seemed so young, so new to love and at such a crossroad in life. I didn't think you were ready. I prayed every day that God would guide your hearts.

I don't know what to pray for today. But I love you both and I believe in you. I pray God will continue to guide you.

If you need me, I am here for you. I will support you, both of you, whatever you choose.

You are two strong, amazing, incredible people.

I'm praying for you and I love you,
Mom Dean

Tears rolled down Theresa's cheeks. The rustle of footsteps in the snow made her turn. She looked up. Alex was standing behind her. His eyes sparkled in the sun. His face was flushed with fatigue and exhaustion, but strength shone in his eyes.

"The cottage community at Cedar Lake sent us notes and money after we called off the wedding." She held some up. "I was just reading one from your mother. It's beautiful."

She slid over. He sat beside her on the bench. He read the letter, then he opened the next one and they kept reading. They sat side by side, their shoulders touching, letters spread across their laps, looking at the remnants of the romance they'd once had.

"I felt like I could never come back here," she said softly. "Like everything had been ruined. I never imagined anyone here was rooting for us. I never dreamed I could come back. I thought I wasn't wanted."

"You were always wanted." Alex's voice was gruff. "I'm just sorry I didn't know how to tell you."

She looked over at him. Then looked down. Her engagement ring, the one he'd given to her so long ago, sat in his hand. He twisted it back and forth in his fingers. He raised the ring in his hands. The diamonds sparkled between his fingers. She felt her heart leap inside her with that same nervous excitement she'd had when he'd dropped to his knees and held it out to her.

"Alex?" Her voice came out in a whisper as his name caught in her throat.

"I never told you," he said, "but you need to know now that I didn't have the money to buy this ring back then. It was way out of my budget. But it was the most beautiful one I'd ever seen, and you were so amazing and so out of my league that I didn't stop myself. So I got a credit card, one of those ones with ridiculously high interest rates, and I maxed it out. So that I could give this to you. Because you deserved the best. You deserved everything. When your dad saw it, he guessed what I'd done. He challenged me on it and told me I shouldn't start a marriage in financial trouble, with a debt like that hanging over me. So he offered to give me cash to cover it. I said I'd pay him back."

He closed his fingers over the ring. It disappeared from the light. "So I'm going to do the right thing now, sell the ring and pay back my debt to your father. I never should've been irresponsible like that. Your parents were in financial trouble, I owed your dad money, this ring had been my gift to you, but I childishly threw it into a corner of the boathouse." He shook his head. He let out a long breath. "I might have loved you with everything I had in me, but I wasn't ready to be the kind of man you needed me to be."

"I wasn't ready, either," she said. "Neither of us were. And I'm sorry I pushed you to be someone different than the man you were so obviously meant to be."

When she was younger she'd thought she'd needed a man to be strong for her, because she doubted her ability to be strong for herself. Now she knew she could be strong. She wanted someone to be strong with. And here he was, everything she had wanted, and more than she'd ever hoped to find when she'd first fallen for him on these shores all those many years ago.

She slid the letters and cards back into the envelopes. "I don't know what my dad will say, but I'm sure he'll be happy to hear from you."

"I'm sorry I hurt you," Alex said.

She smiled. He smiled back.

"I'm sorry I hurt you, too," she said.

His arms slid around her shoulders. She curled into his chest. He hugged her deeply. And for a moment it felt like every broken piece that had been rattling around inside her heart finally settled and clicked back into place.

"Ms. Theresa Vaughan?" A voice called her name. She turned. An officer was standing behind her.

"One moment." She waved at the officer over her shoulder. Then she handed the satchel of letters to Alex. "Can you talk to your parents about this? Tell them we found it. There's a couple thousand dollars in there. It feels wrong to keep it."

"I will take care of it." He took the satchel from her hands. They stood. She knew how this went and what happened next. They both had things to do. In mere moments they'd lose each other in the chaos again.

She took one last look at him, memorizing the rugged lines of his face.

"Thank you," she said. "Hopefully, I'll see you again before we head home to Toronto. But if not, give me a call. It would be great to grab coffee and catch up."

She turned to go.

"Theresa, wait." His hand grabbed hers. She turned back. "I know I wasn't everything you needed and everything you deserved. But I never stopped loving you."

"I never stopped loving you, either." Tears

filled her eyes. "You were all I ever wanted, and I'm so happy to see the person you've become."

Alex pulled her into his arms. She felt his mouth on hers. He kissed her deeply. Her body melted into his and in that moment she knew without a doubt that she was finally back where she belonged. The kiss ended, but still he didn't let her go.

"Can we start over again?" he asked. His hands rested on the small of her back. His intense gaze focused on her face. "I know now that I never should've given up on us."

"Yes." She smiled and felt tears of happiness slip down her cheeks. "I'll never give up on us again."

He kissed her tears away. "Neither will I."

EPILOGUE

Bright spring sun shone through the front window of the windshield of Theresa's car as she navigated it up the narrow highway to Cedar Lake. The last streams of melting snow ran down the rocks in rivulets and sparkled in the morning sunlight. Rivers pulsed and surged.

Winter had ended. Spring was here.

A small, handwritten note sat on her dashboard, with cryptic symbols and hints telling her where to go. It had been sitting in her mailbox at work when she'd left the night before, and the familiar scrawl had sent chills spilling down her spine. She and Alex had had several long conversations over coffees and dinners, and on the phone deep into the night, in the weeks since the terrifying time they'd spent in the storm at Cedar Lake.

Tanner had pled guilty and cut a deal to testify against Emmett, who'd been threatening and blackmailing him for months. Emmett and Kyle had turned on each other, in a hurry to testify against each other. Brick and Howler's bodies had been retrieved, and she'd attended both their funerals. Corey wasn't going to be prosecuted for his role in hiding the videotape of the arson, which Theresa's parents were now using to file a fresh case against the insurance company.

As for her old engagement ring, true to his word, Alex had sold it and taken the money to her father. She didn't know how that conversation had gone. But she trusted him completely. Once she'd fallen in love with the kernel of what she'd thought he could be. Now the full grown man he'd become took her breath away.

Her eyes rose to the clock on the dashboard. The cryptic letter had told her to be at the coordinates in ten minutes' time. She was almost there. Her heart lifted in thankful prayer to God, as her car turned and twisted down the familiar road. Past the Patterson family's cottage. Past her old cottage. Past Joshua's cottage, where her hope chest had been. Past the Dean family's cottage. Past all the cottages that dotted Cedar Lake and onto the rugged, unpaved track. A question burned in her heart. Where was Alex directing her?

The road ended. She pulled to a stop, slid the note into her pocket and stepped out of the car.

A rough path lay ahead of her in the woods, but it was decked with flowers tied onto the trees.

A curious smile curled at the corners of her lips. She tossed her scarf around her neck, slid her hands deep into the pockets of her spring jacket and followed them. The path wove through the woods. Then the trees parted. The beautiful sparkling blue of Cedar Lake spread out beneath her.

In front of it stood Alex.

His mouth turned up in a crooked grin that sent shivers down her spine. Sunlight shone down on the strong lines of his form. A smile illuminated his face as her eyes met his.

"What is this?" she asked. "Where are we?"

"Our own piece of Cedar Lake." His arms spread wide, taking in the untamed woods pressing in on either side and the glittering lake beyond. "It was owned by the Pattersons. But I spoke to them this week. They're willing to let us buy it to build our own cottage. Your parents gave me their blessing to use the money from the ring as the deposit. The rest I made up from my savings, plus the money in the envelopes. I've spoken to every family who gave us money for the wedding, and they're all on board with us adding a twelfth cottage to the lake. If we want." His voice dropped. "If this is what you want."

If this was what she wanted? If she wanted her own piece of Cedar Lake? If she wanted to share it with Alex? Was this some kind of dream? "It would be ours?"

"Ours." He stepped toward her and took her hands. "Yours and mine. Our own cottage on the lake, built together, with our own hands and our own design, to spend our summers in as a family whenever it's done, whenever we're ready to take that step."

Alex knelt on the rock. His fingers opened. There sat a ring, a simple band of gold flecked with three small diamonds.

"It will take months to develop this property into something livable and build a cottage here," he said. "This is a long-term project. And it will take us time, too, to build the kind of strong foundation to our relationship that I know we both want it to have. But I love you, Theresa. I always have and I always will. You are worth waiting for. Will you marry me?"

"Yes!" Happiness leaped in her heart and danced in her eyes. "Yes, I will marry you. Yes, I will build my future with you."

"You said yes?" Joy filled his eyes.

"I said yes!"

Then, before he could ask again, she grabbed his hands and pulled him up. He slid the ring onto her finger. Her lips met his. Then his arms wrapped around her waist, pulling her up off her feet and into his embrace.

They kissed again, with the promise of forever, on the edge of Cedar Lake.

* * * * *

If you enjoyed
RESCUE AT CEDAR LAKE,
look for these other books
by Maggie K. Black:

KIDNAPPED AT CHRISTMAS
TACTICAL RESCUE
HEADLINE: MURDER

Dear Reader,

Ever since I was a teenager, my favorite author has been Madeleine L'Engle. When I was just starting out as a writer, I drove to Illinois to visit her archives at Wheaton College. There I sat in a beautiful book-lined room and read through the earliest drafts of my favorite novels, with their typewriter smudges and editorial lines. She was the first author I ever read whose characters crossed between books, with their lives unfolding in other people's stories.

When I wrote Alex and Theresa into *Kidnapped at Christmas*, I just knew I had to continue their story and help them find their happily-ever-after.

I should add a quick thank-you to the Taylor family for letting me rent their cottage in the summer, which formed the inspiration for this story. The Cedar Lake in this book is entirely fictional, though, and not inspired by any one of over a dozen Cedar Lakes that do exist in Ontario. Thank you also to all of you who've posted reviews of my past books and written to me with your thoughts and comments. As always, you can find me online at www.maggiekblack.com or on Twitter at @maggiekblack.

Thank you for sharing the journey,
Maggie Black

LARGER-PRINT BOOKS!

GET 2 FREE LARGER-PRINT NOVELS PLUS 2 FREE MYSTERY GIFTS

Love Inspired®

Larger-print novels are now available...

YES! Please send me 2 FREE LARGER-PRINT Love Inspired® novels and my 2 FREE mystery gifts (gifts are worth about $10). After receiving them, if I don't wish to receive any more books, I can return the shipping statement marked "cancel." If I don't cancel, I will receive 6 brand-new novels every month and be billed just $5.49 per book in the U.S. or $5.99 per book in Canada. That's a savings of at least 19% off the cover price. It's quite a bargain! Shipping and handling is just 50¢ per book in the U.S. and 75¢ per book in Canada.* I understand that accepting the 2 free books and gifts places me under no obligation to buy anything. I can always return a shipment and cancel at any time. Even if I never buy another book, the two free books and gifts are mine to keep forever.

122/322 IDN GH6D

Name	(PLEASE PRINT)	
Address		Apt. #
City	State/Prov.	Zip/Postal Code

Signature (if under 18, a parent or guardian must sign)

Mail to the **Reader Service:**
IN U.S.A.: P.O. Box 1867, Buffalo, NY 14240-1867
IN CANADA: P.O. Box 609, Fort Erie, Ontario L2A 5X3

**Are you a current subscriber to Love Inspired® books and want to receive the larger-print edition?
Call 1-800-873-8635 or visit www.ReaderService.com.**

* Terms and prices subject to change without notice. Prices do not include applicable taxes. Sales tax applicable in N.Y. Canadian residents will be charged applicable taxes. Offer not valid in Quebec. This offer is limited to one order per household. Not valid to current subscribers to Love Inspired Larger-Print books. All orders subject to credit approval. Credit or debit balances in a customer's account(s) may be offset by any other outstanding balance owed by or to the customer. Please allow 4 to 6 weeks for delivery. Offer available while quantities last.

Your Privacy—The Reader Service is committed to protecting your privacy. Our Privacy Policy is available online at www.ReaderService.com or upon request from the Reader Service.

We make a portion of our mailing list available to reputable third parties that offer products we believe may interest you. If you prefer that we not exchange your name with third parties, or if you wish to clarify or modify your communication preferences, please visit us at www.ReaderService.com/consumerchoice or write to us at Reader Service Preference Service, P.O. Box 9062, Buffalo, NY 14240-9062. Include your complete name and address.

LILP15

REQUEST YOUR FREE BOOKS!
2 FREE WHOLESOME ROMANCE NOVELS
IN LARGER PRINT
PLUS 2
FREE
MYSTERY GIFTS

🌸🌸🌸🌸🌸🌸🌸🌸🌸🌸🌸🌸🌸🌸🌸🌸🌸🌸🌸

HEARTWARMING™

🌺🌺🌺🌺🌺🌺🌺🌺🌺🌺🌺🌺🌺🌺🌺🌺🌺🌺🌺

Wholesome, tender romances

YES! Please send me 2 FREE Harlequin® Heartwarming Larger-Print novels and my 2 FREE mystery gifts (gifts worth about $10). After receiving them, if I don't wish to receive any more books, I can return the shipping statement marked "cancel." If I don't cancel, I will receive 4 brand-new larger-print novels every month and be billed just $5.24 per book in the U.S. or $5.99 per book in Canada. That's a savings of at least 19% off the cover price. It's quite a bargain! Shipping and handling is just 50¢ per book in the U.S. and 75¢ per book in Canada.* I understand that accepting the 2 free books and gifts places me under no obligation to buy anything. I can always return a shipment and cancel at any time. Even if I never buy another book, the two free books and gifts are mine to keep forever.

161/361 IDN GHX2

Name	(PLEASE PRINT)	
Address		Apt. #
City	State/Prov.	Zip/Postal Code

Signature (if under 18, a parent or guardian must sign)

Mail to the **Reader Service:**
IN U.S.A.: P.O. Box 1867, Buffalo, NY 14240-1867
IN CANADA: P.O. Box 609, Fort Erie, Ontario L2A 5X3

* Terms and prices subject to change without notice. Prices do not include applicable taxes. Sales tax applicable in N.Y. Canadian residents will be charged applicable taxes. Offer not valid in Quebec. This offer is limited to one order per household. Not valid for current subscribers to Harlequin Heartwarming larger-print books. All orders subject to credit approval. Credit or debit balances in a customer's account(s) may be offset by any other outstanding balance owed by or to the customer. Please allow 4 to 6 weeks for delivery. Offer available while quantities last.

Your Privacy—The Reader Service is committed to protecting your privacy. Our Privacy Policy is available online at www.ReaderService.com or upon request from the Reader Service.

We make a portion of our mailing list available to reputable third parties that offer products we believe may interest you. If you prefer that we not exchange your name with third parties, or if you wish to clarify or modify your communication preferences, please visit us at www.ReaderService.com/consumerchoice or write to us at Reader Service Preference Service, P.O. Box 9062, Buffalo, NY 14240-9062. Include your complete name and address.

WESTERN WP PROMISES

YES! Please send me **The Western Promises Collection** in Larger Print. This collection begins with 3 FREE books and 2 FREE gifts (gifts valued at approx. $14.00 retail) in the first shipment, along with the other first 4 books from the collection! If I do not cancel, I will receive 8 monthly shipments until I have the entire 51-book Western Promises collection. I will receive 2 or 3 FREE books in each shipment and I will pay just $4.99 US/ $5.89 CDN for each of the other four books in each shipment, plus $2.99 for shipping and handling per shipment. *If I decide to keep the entire collection, I'll have paid for only 32 books, because 19 books are FREE! I understand that accepting the 3 free books and gifts places me under no obligation to buy anything. I can always return a shipment and cancel at any time. My free books and gifts are mine to keep no matter what I decide.

272 HCN 3070 472 HCN 3070

Name	(PLEASE PRINT)	
Address		Apt. #
City	State/Prov.	Zip/Postal Code

Signature (if under 18, a parent or guardian must sign)

Mail to the **Reader Service:**

IN U.S.A.: P.O. Box 1867, Buffalo, NY 14240-1867
IN CANADA: P.O. Box 609, Fort Erie, Ontario L2A 5X3

READERSERVICE.COM

Manage your account online!

- Review your order history
- Manage your payments
- Update your address

> ### *We've designed the Reader Service website just for you.*

Enjoy all the features!

- Discover new series available to you, and read excerpts from any series.
- Respond to mailings and special monthly offers.
- Browse the Bonus Bucks catalog and online-only exculsives.
- Share your feedback.

Visit us at:

ReaderService.com

RS16R